THE MARQUIS AND THE MAGICIAN'S ASSISTANT

THE REBEL ROYALS BOOK 4

SHANAE JOHNSON

THOSE JOHNSON GIRLS

"Ladies and gentleman," called the young, fresh-faced man in a top hat and tails. "I, the Great Blaze Mercury, will astound you with an age-old trick, the skill most desired by men, and that is to saw a woman in half."

There were a few catcalls and whoops from the skeleton audience in the theater. It wasn't showtime, just a rehearsal. As the show's financial backer and producer, Omar al Shariff, the Marquis of Navarre of the island nation of Córdoba, settled into the cushions of the couch just off stage. He had a front row seat to the actual action. As he'd learned in these last couple of weeks since he'd taken a step into the wondrous world of magic, the real action happened behind the curtain.

Just off to the side of the stage, a tiny brunette heaved a weary sigh before she took beleaguered steps towards the baby-faced magician. She had a dancer's body and grace. Her long, brown locks were swept up high on her head, but a few tendrils escaped the coiled bun to caress her swan's neck. She swayed like a willow dancing on a light breeze as she made her way across the stage. She had elongated limbs that ended in perfectly arched points, whether they be her arched toes in satin heels or her elegant fingers that fanned out as she spread her arms when she came up beside the magician.

"My assistant, the beautiful and sexy Lark Voorheen here will step into this box," said Mercury the Great. He held out his hand to the magician's assistant. Lark gave the man a death glare and stepped around his proffered hand.

Omar grinned at the fire in her eyes and the bladed edge of that tight smile. He knew the woman's wit was sharp, and her tongue could cut a man into a thousand tiny pieces before he knew that man was in trouble. The magician was in trouble.

"You know you're setting Women's Liberation back with your cheesy jokes and this even cheesier trick," came Lark's biting pronouncement. "Our worth is already calculated at less than the value of a man's. Now you want to cut me in half?"

The magician bit his upper lip, revealing unnaturally straight teeth that could have only been the result of years of orthodontic intervention. His Adam's apple worked up and down, like the gears of a broken clock trying to figure out if the time on the dial indicated whether it was day or night. Finally, the young man laughed. But it came out like the sound of a scared hyena.

"That time of the month, my dear?" And then the fool had the audacity to pat her hands before turning to address the audience. "Don't worry, everyone. No blood will be spilled."

Omar was certain the subtle change in Lark's face could be seen from the back of the theater. The inner corner of her catlike eyes narrowed ever so slightly. That perfectly, heart-shaped mouth pinched just at the divot in the center, making her lips even more plump and rounded.

If it wasn't clear to the peanut gallery in the audience before, it was clear to everyone in the room that the magician was in serious trouble. The magician's assistant's mouth smoothed out into a smile so sweet and captivating that the Great Mercury gasped. A few other men in the seats gasped as well; a slight, swift intake of breath that said loud and clear *I'm under your spell.*

Omar felt a sharp thud in his chest. He'd gasped too. He'd already known he was in trouble from the first moment he saw that woman.

Lark stepped into the cheap plywood box that would render her in two. The magician went about putting in the stocks that would hold her head and feet in place. He chattered on while he went about his preparations.

Omar wasn't paying attention to him anymore. No one in the theater was. All attention was rapt on the woman whose gaze hadn't ceased its calculating gleam since she'd arrived on the stage.

The buzzing of a saw sounded. It began to lower toward Lark. The blade hit the top of the box, and wood splinters began to fly. Then the wrenching sound of gears was like a record scratch on the performance. The blade sped up.

"Wait, that's not supposed to happen." The magician fumbled with the blade. But he couldn't stop the sharp wheel from spinning. Splinters flew faster, farther.

"Turn it off, you idiot," said Lark. Her calculating

eyes now filled with terror as the splinters made way for the blade to pierce her flesh.

A second later, Lark's pretty mouth opened on a scream. A different gasp went through the audience, one of uncertainty. Omar leaped from the comfort of the couch just as the blade hit pay dirt.

Red splattered from the crevices of the wood box. Men rushed to the stage. Omar was just at the edge of the curtain when Lark slipped out of the box.

Her long limbs were attached. Her torso was an unblemished hourglass. Her hands were in the air, fingers fanning in a pose of *ta-dah*.

"Relax," she crooned, sending the audience a wink. "I'm good. It's him you need to worry about." Lark turned and shoved the magician into the open box.

"What most people don't understand about magic is that it's all an illusion," Lark continued. With a few flicks of her wrist, she had Mercury secured. Ignoring the man's protests, she reset the blade and aimed it for his torso. "Magician's wave their hands and shout silly words all to distract. Meanwhile, it's the assistant that does all the work."

The blade made its way through the magician's body. Lark began to pull the box apart but stopped.

"Oh, right, say the magic word."

The audience, now assured of her safety and apparently not caring about the magician's fate said the word; *abracadabra*.

Lark leaned against the box, speaking conversationally and completely unconcerned about the mutilated man in the box. "Do you know that even that word is believed to be sexist? *Ab* is Hebrew for father. *Ben* means son. I'm telling you, it's like they were asking for it."

She pulled apart the box with a flourish to reveal that the magician was, in fact, sawed in half.

The small crowd roared with approval, and Omar knew he had a hit on his hand. A magic show where the female assistant was the star. When Lark had brought the idea to him a few weeks ago, he hadn't immediately seen its potential. Admittedly, he'd been far too distracted by the woman's legs. But he couldn't afford another distraction in his life.

Omar had a rule. He didn't date performers. Especially ones that worked for him. Anymore.

And so he'd kept his distance. In his personal life. But in matters of business, it was clear to see that Lark, a former magician's assistant herself, was pure magic.

Her show had everything. Glitz, glamor, humor,

and a beautiful woman outsmarting a bumbling man. It was going to be a hit! Not only that but working with such a beautiful woman and not having any romantic ties would restore his reputation in the industry.

In his long career, Omar had dated exactly one woman whom he'd brought into the spotlight. And it had been a glaring disaster. But public perception would've made anyone believe he'd dated an entire chorus line. It was not a good look for business, especially in a day and age where predators were being outed from the casting couch.

Omar rose from his place on the backstage couch. He was not that kind of producer. He was not that kind of man. With his dark good looks, a noble title, and old money, he had no need to prey on women. Aside from all that, his mother had raised him to respect women above others.

"She's pretty."

Omar's hackles raised at the sound of that husky voice. His legs felt weary, and he sat back down. He might have been taught to respect all women. But he wasn't fool enough to give respect back to a woman who had none for herself or others.

"What are you doing here, Summer?" Omar turned to face his ex.

Summer Briggs had the same long and lean form as Lark. But she was more lines than curves, which meant there was nothing much to hold onto. After Omar had given her a boost up onto the stage, she'd slipped through his fingers. And then to add insult to injury, she'd stepped on the hands that had lifted her up.

"Just checking out the competition," said Summer. "You said we could still be friends."

"No, you said that. I don't think we ever were friends."

"Well, let's start now. Let's go out. I was thinking we would have a great time together at the royal wedding."

Oh. So, that's what this was about. She wasn't checking out Lark's show. Summer didn't believe she had any competition. But she also didn't have a way into the highly anticipated, extremely exclusive, invite-only wedding of the King of Córdoba and his American bride. One did have to have friends to get one of the coveted invitations. As one of King Leo's oldest and closest friends, Omar was the first to get one.

"Sorry, Summer. My invitation says plus one, and you subtracted yourself from my life when you broke your contract to sign with Rancik Entertainment."

Omar didn't mention that she'd broken his heart as well as their contract. He had truly believed that Summer cared for him. She was a fine actress.

Summer pouted her lips, preparing another award-winning performance. She plopped down on his lap and wrapped her arms around his neck.

Omar turned away and came face to face with his new rising star.

"Sorry," said Lark, lifting an eyebrow as she regarded him. "I'll come back later."

"No, not at all." Omar stood, displacing Summer off to the side of the couch. "We were done long ago."

Lark lifted the other brow at him.

Omar thought it best not to try to explain any further. "I'm working here, Summer. Do you mind?"

Summer brushed her skirt off and stood. Her shrewd gaze took Lark in. "Enjoy the ride while it lasts, honey. He'll discard you the second he's done with you."

Omar wanted to protest. Not only was Summer the only one in his employment he'd ever dated, but she was also the one who had left him.

"He could try," said Lark. "But I know magic. I'm very good at hiding bodies."

Omar chuckled. Yeah, Lark was a perfect distraction. He'd already forgotten Summer's presence. His full attention was on Lark.

"Have a seat," he said to her, indicating the spot next to him on the couch.

CHAPTER TWO

*L*arked eyed the empty space on the couch. There was still a slight indent in it from where the last woman had landed after Omar had tossed her aside.

Instead of sitting, Lark stayed right where she was. She stood with her knees pressed together, her arms crossed over her chest, and her chin high. Even though he sat, Omar was still eye level with her.

Omar was a tall man; tall, dark, and handsome. He was truly the most beautifully put together man she'd ever seen in her life. And she'd been a dancer amongst some of the prettiest men in the world. If that weren't enough, he was also rich and titled.

Omar oozed with the power of an ancient sheik with the aristocratic manners of a Victorian gentleman.

The Marquis of Navarre looked as though he'd just walked out of the desert and into civilization. His sun-kissed skin was somewhere between bronze and golden even in the dim backstage fluorescents. His dark gaze fairly gleamed as he regarded her, chuckling at Lark's set down of the woman who was storming, rather loudly, off the stage.

Those eyes of his, sometimes hazel brown, other times honey golden, challenged Lark as he patted the empty seat. Tiger's eyes; that was the stone they reminded her of. It was also the predator the marquis made her think of.

The man was dangerous with his sleek beauty and his toothsome grin. But Lark knew better than to get too close. And so she stayed off the couch and away from the man.

"Sorry about that," Omar said.

Lark had to take a deep breath. Even his voice reached out to her, trying to curl its talons around her and urge her closer to him. She took a step but only to plant her feet in a wide stance to hold her ground.

"Former client," Omar continued.

"She thought she could still have company benefits?"

Instead of wincing in anger, Omar's bright gaze sparked with surprise. He threw his head back and let out another laugh. A hearty and full one this time. Lark caught sight of a few dark bristles just beneath his chin. The tiny hairs were trying to climb up that strong jaw.

She didn't blame them their path. Just beyond his jaw rested the lushest set of lips Lark had yet to encounter. Those were claiming lips; a full bottom lip that would take a woman's entire mouth if she wasn't careful.

Lark shook herself, reminding herself to be careful around this man. But she was growing weary from the internal struggle. She took a few tentative steps forward and sat at the farthest edge of the couch. It didn't matter. Omar's presence was so big that even though there was a cushion between them, the sheer heat of him crept over her, like the rays of the sun on a hot summer's day.

He stretched his arm along the backside of the couch. His fingertips could've brushed her shoulder, making it so far as to touch the loose tendrils of hair at the nape of her neck. But he didn't. He kept his hands to himself.

Lark couldn't discern if she was pleased with his deference or disappointed by his restraint. Omar al Shariff had her in a precarious situation. He had agreed to back her show. The terms of the agreement were very fair. And, so far, he'd given her the leeway to run the show as she'd envisioned.

She had to be missing something. He had to be up to something. At any moment, the other shoe was going to drop.

"I can't believe that's the opening you came up with," he said.

And so it began ...

"I was out of my seat, even though you told me what was going to happen," he continued. His predator's eyes shone with wonder and awe as he gazed down at her. "This is going to be a hit."

That was it? He liked it? He wasn't going to make any changes? Lark was at a loss.

She was used to being shoved into boxes by men. She was used to them throwing darts and just barely missing some vital organ on her person. And now she sat, on a couch in the back of a theater, with no one else around, and the producer sang her praises and kept his hands to himself. In fact, he had never made a pass at her since the first day they'd met.

Lark had been trying to peg him since she'd seen him lounging bar side on a luxury yacht. Even while relaxing, he'd brought to mind a panther, always at the ready to strike. But Lark had struck first.

She'd known who he was; one of Europe's most influential and successful entertainment producers. He had made many a career. He was also notorious for dating his female starlets.

While staying at the home of the Duke of Mondego with her best friend, Lark had put on an impromptu show. The marquis had quirked a regal brow at her performance and handed her his card. She'd taken that card and ran with it. This was her shot, her chance to do magic on her own terms. She was not going to blow it because her new boss was hotter than the sun.

"Do you think the full show will be ready by the end of the month?" he asked.

"Absolutely. Just a few more days of rehearsal and we'll be good to go."

"I'm glad to hear it."

He turned to her. When he did so, his hand brushed her shoulder cap. Lark jerked out of his reach, but not before a sizzling shudder went down her spine and curled her toes.

Here it was. The come on. She was ready for it.

Omar lifted his hand up in a stop-motion. He grinned at her. Lark made sure to note the sharpness of his white teeth. Those canines would lure a lesser woman in and tear her apart. Luckily, Lark was made of stronger stuff.

"Despite what you just saw, you should know that I don't date talent."

Lark was unmoved. It was how they all began, playing the abstinence card. And then, when they made their move, she was led to feel special that they made an exception for her. That was before they took a bite out of her.

"You have a lot of talent," Omar continued. "And I think you know it."

This talk was not going the way she'd expected. In fact, nothing about this man was as she'd expected. He kept surprising her at every turn. And he was spinning her around again.

"You've been overlooked and undervalued your entire career. Not any longer. We're going to make magic together, Ms. Voorheen. Although we should do something about that last name. It doesn't roll off the tongue."

"I'm not changing my last name." She shrugged. "Family pride."

Truth be told, her father went by a different

stage name. Her sister was married with a new hyphenated name. The name didn't truly have real significance to her. She just wanted to see if she could win a fight with this man on a low-level point of disagreement.

Omar nodded slowly. Then he shrugged. "Fine. I can live with that."

He reached his hand forward. Lark leaned back, assuming it was aiming for her breast. But it stopped short, aiming more to the right, near her heart. Oh, he certainly was a dangerous man.

She clasped her hand in his. His long fingers curled around hers, caging her in. She squeezed right back, hard and firm as her father had taught her. Omar gave her hand a shake that threatened to rattle loose her forearm from its socket.

"Did you see that?" he asked.

"See what?"

"Sparkles."

In the air between them, shimmering down onto the fleshy part of where their hands met were tiny twinkles of brilliance.

"Oh," she said. "Those are from my costume."

Omar was still holding her hand. But she was still holding his. Slowly, their fingers uncurled from each other.

Lark stood, brushing her costume off. More sparkles filled the air between them. She paid them no heed. On steady feet, she headed for the dressing room.

This was good. She had gotten everything she wanted, and she hadn't had to strike any wrists with her magic wand or toss a throwing dagger at private areas. It was the best business arrangement she'd ever had. Heck, it was the best relationship she'd ever been in. Now, she just had to keep her libido under control.

CHAPTER THREE

Omar loved the finer things in life. He had expensive tastes but not caviar dreams. That particular delicacy was simply an appetizer.

Omar loved exclusive cars that swaggered down the street before he stepped out of the door. He sipped vintage wines that were older than some present-day countries. But mostly, he loved tailored clothes.

He was not an off-the-rack kind of man. His closet was filled with fabrics where each stitch was sewn together with only him in mind.

"You're going to need another fitting."

Omar took a slow and deep breath at those words. The breath was slow and careful because he'd had to take in a number of deep breaths the hour he'd been in the fitting room. Another swift inhale and he was likely to pass out.

"Have you stopped working out?" Leonidas Almeria, beloved King of Córdoba, Omar's most trusted and oldest friend, and the groomzilla from hell walked a circuit around Omar. The king's nose was scrunched in distaste. His gaze was narrowed in displeasure. "I could've sworn you were a bigger size?"

Omar counted to ten. Then to twenty. Right then, he wished he were a bridesmaid. He could hear the bride, Esme, and the girls giggling in the next room. Meanwhile, Omar, Prince Alexander, and Daniel, the Earl of Larida, were trapped with His Majestic Pain in the Derrière.

"Did you get the changes to the menu?" Leo directed this question to his brother.

"Yes, Leo." Alex's voice was dispassionate when he answered. His attention was focused on his phone screen.

Omar knew the man was unlikely to be scrolling the headlines or playing a game. A glance in the reflective mirror showed that Alex was indeed looking at pictures of exotic dishes. The prince had had an obsession with food since he'd learned to hold a knife and fork.

"Esme really likes apple pies, and I want her to have only the best."

That brought Alex's attention up. "Esme loves Jan's pies, in particular, Jan's Poison Apple Pie."

"But Jan's not baking the pies," said Leo.

"Because she's the Maid of Honor and she's already planned the entire menu, is cooking for the rehearsal dinner, and is having to put up with you changing things every other second. I won't have you run my fiancée into the ground and have her consider running away from this crazy family before I can get a ring on her finger."

"Fair point." Leo sighed as though he were entirely inconvenienced. "I wouldn't want to upset Jan. Esme would have my head if her best friend were unhappy."

The three men in the room looked at the king of the realm. At every turn, Leo had asked each of them to go above, beyond, and then an inch further in the preparations for his second wedding. As the day drew nearer, his demands tested the bounds of diva-ness.

"Daniel ..." Leo turned to the quiet man of the bunch.

As usual, the earl's head was buried behind the covers of a thick, hardback book. At the sound of his name, Daniel did not put the book down. He calmly turned the page, the only acknowledgment that the man was still breathing.

"Daniel, I need you to take another look at my vows," said Leo.

"What's wrong with the new draft?" Came the muffled voice from behind the covers.

"It's not ..." Leo waved his hands in the air, searching for the right words, "romantic enough."

The pages rustled as Daniel's fingers stiffened. The gold embossed title of the book read *The Complete, Unabridged Works of Jane Austen*. The cover of the book slid down to reveal bright green eyes that darkened a few shades as Daniel regarded his king.

"Not romantic enough?" Each of the three words was clipped and enunciated with disbelief.

"No," said Leo. He was looking up at the ceiling for his words now and not at the murderous gaze of the bibliophile. Since the very real possibility of regicide wasn't on Leo's mind, the monarch kept going. "Can't you find a quote or something in one of your books? But not Austen, she's far too rigid and unrealistic. Something from a fairytale like Grimm or Seuss."

Omar was still on the platform with the tailor

poking needles and thread through his clothing, so he would not have gotten to the earl in time. Luckily, Alex was quick on his feet. He got to Daniel before the man could take a step to Leo with that twenty-pound hardback weapon raised to strike. Omar wasn't sure if Alex saved his brother's life out of fraternal devotion or because the prince had no desire to rule.

In Leo's defense, the man was over the moon in love and eager to marry his bride. He had had no hand in his first wedding plans. He hadn't even chosen the bride.

In truth, Esme hadn't even been Leo's first choice as a second wife. But she'd wound up being his only choice. It was no wonder he wanted everything perfect for her.

"Omar." Leo turned back to him.

Omar took another slow, deep breath as the king's attention turned back to him. Omar had eagerly accepted the role of Best Man at Leo's wedding. The first time had been a breeze as everything was planned for the man who would be king. Today, it was a different story as the man who was king took a hands-on approach in running his country and his personal life.

Omar braced himself for the next missive. What

would it be this time? Would Leo want Omar to drive down to the florist growing the wedding flowers to check on their progress? Again?

"You still haven't RSVP'd your plus one," said Leo.

"You'll be a handful enough on the big day." With the jacket measurements done, Omar slipped off the garment and handed it back to the tailor. "I'm not bringing anyone."

"You can't do that," protested Leo. "You have to bring someone, or the seating arrangements will be unbalanced."

Omar's lungs protested the excess air he tried to force past his throat. Instead, he walked to the door.

"Oy," called Daniel. "Where are you going?"

"Do not leave us alone with him," said Alex.

Leo looked between the three of them with surprise, as though he had no clue what the three closest men in his life could possibly be referring to.

"I just need to ask Jan something," said Omar.

"I probably know the answer," said Alex.

"It's a Maid of Honor-Best Man thing," Omar called out over his shoulder as he walked out the door.

He could hear Alex grumble as the door shut. Omar felt no remorse. It was survival of the fittest in this animal kingdom. And besides, his dating life was not up for debate. He was off the market, had been for a while since Summer had pulled the curtains out from under him.

Omar saw no reason to date or even marry. Laws were being changed in the country which would free him from the burden of producing a male heir to pass his title onto. Once those laws were passed, and women could take on the titles and the responsibilities, Omar had every intention of abdicating.

His older sister was already performing all the responsibilities of the marquisate. Alana was far more interested in and far better at, noble affairs than Omar could or would ever be. She ran the family empire while he'd built his own in entertainment. If things went the way Omar expected they would go in the parliament, he expected he would live as a bachelor for the rest of his days.

Omar knocked on the door to the ladies' fitting room. The door opened, but he had to look way down until he met the gaze of the little girl standing guard in the doorway.

"Hi, Uncle Omar."

"Hello there, Princess Pea."

Omar reached down and lifted Penelope up into his arms. She was dressed in a light pink tool that fluttered as he spun her around. He didn't spin her as fast as he had in the past. The little princess was getting big.

"Don't tell me," came a voice from the interior. "He's being unbearable again."

Omar entered to see Esme standing on a platform. She was a vision in white. There were sparkles on the dress, making her twinkle like a star. But nothing outshined the look of love coming through her eyes and fairly oozing out of her pores. Leo was a lucky man.

"I can't blame him," said Omar. "He's close to marrying the woman of his dreams. You are a dream come true, Esmeralda."

Esme blushed, her red cheeks stark with all the white cloth. "Your dream girl is out there somewhere."

"I can wait," said Omar.

All around him, nobles were falling like flies. Leo was marrying Esme. Alex was engaged to Jan. And then there was Alex's best friend, the Duke of Mondego. Omar was certain Zhi would pop the question to his girlfriend, Spin, any day now.

"Hey, I just realized," said Esme. "You haven't RSVP'd your plus one."

Great. He'd walked out of the frying pan and right into the fire.

"You're not bringing that actress, what's her name?" asked Jan. The pie maker sat on a plush couch in jeans and a t-shirt, sipping a pink drink.

"Summer," said Esme.

"I didn't like her," said Penelope.

"She doesn't eat chocolate," said Jan. "Who doesn't eat chocolate?"

"I'm not seeing her anymore," said Omar.

"Or that singer," said Esme. "She barely spoke above a whisper."

Omar hadn't dated Carlie Hyland. But because he'd produced her and they'd been seen out getting dinner a few times, the public assumed they had something else going on.

"Or that model who was a vegetarian," said Jan. "She cried when the meat course was brought out."

Corrine Michaels wasn't on Omar's roster. They'd simply sat next to each other at an event and were photographed together, which of course meant they were dating in the eyes of society.

"I'm not bringing anyone to the wedding."

The two women and one tween gaped at him. Even the seamstress stayed her needle.

"I'm not dating anyone right now," said Omar. "I'm focused on work."

It sounded lame to his own ears. But it was the truth. And it didn't hurt that the woman he was currently working with was not only a pleasure to work with but to also look at.

"What about Spin's friend, Lark?" asked Esme. "She's just your type."

She sure was his type. But he reminded himself that he wouldn't touch. He didn't need another Summer fiasco or to be linked with any woman he produced. No, it would be all work and no play when it came to this wedding and Lark Voorheen.

CHAPTER FOUR

"What did you say?"

The response to the question came back garbled. It was mixed and blended into the cacophony of sounds coming from every direction, corner, and nook of the great house of the Mondegos. In the ballroom, spin tables had been set up, and an army of would-be disc jockeys were spinning vinyl and learning to scratch needles. In the former ladies' retiring room, three female and one male soprano were vying for the highest note on the scales. In the front receiving room, four grand pianos were set up with two students on each bench. The young pianists took turns running scales under the direction of the patriarch of the house.

Diego Zhi Wen de Bernadino, Duke of Mondego, stood in the center of the square made by the string instruments. His hands were raised like a conductor as he led his pupils. But when his gaze fell to the door and spied Spin and Lark in the entryway, he paused. A huge grin split his handsome face as he took in Spin. Even though the ray of love didn't shine on Lark, its effects couldn't be ignored.

Lark had never had a man look at her the way Zhi looked at her best friend. Sure, men ogled her when she was on a stage, or even just walking down a street. But looking at her with a light of utter devotion wanting nothing but her presence, no one would've ever believed that was possible. But here she was seeing proof of it.

"What did you say, my darling?" Zhi repeated. His hands lowered now that the music had stopped, but they didn't drop to his sides. They reached out for Spin as he came near her. He didn't need to come closer to hear her now that there was silence. Lark was certain the man simply couldn't resist the opportunity to take Spin into his arms.

"I said the piano tuner is here," Spin answered as she came willingly into his embrace.

DJ Spin d'Elle, less commonly known by her true name, Lady Eleanor Trent, had never been a woman to hold still or reveal her secrets. Not even to her best friend. But that had all changed when she'd met the duke. Now Spin wrapped her arms around her boyfriend's neck. There was nothing unsaid between the two of them.

"Not in front of the children, you two." Nian Zhen, the dowager duchess, *tsked* from the doorway.

Zhi planted a chaste kiss on Spin's cheek. Then he turned his head and whispered something into her ear. Whatever it was, it made the DJ blush and bite her lip. Spin couldn't hide the fact that she was head over turntables for the duke.

Turning to the children, Zhi said, "You lot, off to an early lunch. We'll pick up on this lesson tomorrow."

The kids filed out into the great hall and headed toward the kitchen as the tuners came in. The tuners weren't the only workers in residence that afternoon. The ducal estate of Mondego House had been transformed into a music and arts school in just a couple of months. Plumbers clanged on pipes. Carpenters beat a percussive tune with hammers. It all mixed in with the kids rapping out back and the dancers tapping on the hardwood floors of the hallway.

It was all euphonious chaos, and Lark loved it. This was how she'd grown up, in a huge, boisterous extended family where quiet was unheard of, and solitude didn't exist. Running the show was the once quiet and reserved dowager duchess.

Nian flitted amongst the children with a grin that never left her face. Her eyes were bright as she stopped to watch performances. Each time she stopped to give encouragement or correction, she clasped her hands to her heart as though she were giving each student a piece of that organ.

When Lark and Spin and first come to Mondego House, the Duchess had been a shell. Now that she was freed from the burden of her abusive husband, she had filled, like sand inside of a clam that opened to produce a pearl.

"My darling girl," Nian said, taking Lark's hands in her own and clasping them to her heart. "You haven't told me how your show with Omar is coming along."

"It's going really great," said Lark. "He hasn't tried to make a single change to my plan. He's letting me put on my exact vision."

"Well, of course, he is. Omar knows talent when he sees it. He's always been great at polishing rough edges. He's lucked out with you because you don't have any."

Lark preened under Nian's praise like she was one of her students. It wasn't only the praise that pleased her. It was the mention of her producer and his belief in her talent. Being of the same noble class, Nian would have known Omar for much of his life. So, she'd have some insight into how the man thought. Lark wanted to believe that she was different than the other acts Omar had produced; that she was something special.

"I met one of his former acts today," Lark hedged.

"Oh, don't tell me it was that Summer woman." Nian curled her lip in distaste.

Lark had never seen the duchess look at anything or anyone with contempt. Not even her husband, who had been cruel to her their entire marriage. "So, you don't like that Summer woman?"

"A man in Omar's position has many women, and a few men, trying to offer him more than their artistic talents if you know what I mean."

Lark knew what she meant. The entertainment industry had bad apples on both sides of the couch. The producers and directors who tried to get talent to sit down with them on the piece of furniture. And the talent who flopped down there on their backs without invitation.

"Omar is usually very good at seeing through those who only want to use him. But for some reason, he didn't see it with Summer."

"She used him to get ahead?"

Nian nodded. "And then, once he'd brought her out into the world and made her relevant, she left him for another producer. He was devastated. I believe he had actual feelings for the minx."

Had he looked devastated the other day when Lark had caught the two backstage? She wasn't entirely sure what she'd walked up on. All she knew was that Omar hadn't tried to make a pass at her, and he seemed to genuinely believe in her talent. It was enough.

One of the longtime housemaids made their way over to the two of them. Thinking it was business with the repairs or the school, Lark prepared to make her excuses. But the maid approached her.

"Ms. Lark, there's a gentleman for you at the door."

Lark frowned. She hadn't met any gentlemen in Córdoba other than Omar. And he'd been welcome in Mondego House since before they'd met. Omar would've simply shown himself in and found her if he needed her for anything. Since the busy marquis didn't need her for anything, it couldn't be him.

Lark moved toward the entryway. Her feet stopped as she saw who the gentleman caller was. The man was no gentleman.

"There you are." Piers Northwood, The Great Nitwitini. His voice was whiny and nasally. "You disappeared on me."

"That was in my job description." Lark eyed the thick drapes on the windows of the entryway. They would make the perfect prop for a disappearing act. "What do you want, Piers?"

"Why, I want you, of course."

He came to her, reaching for her hands. Much in the same way that Zhi had reached for Spin's. Lark put her hands behind her back. Piers was such a mediocre magician that he might actually believe she'd made her hands disappear. But no such luck. He rested his hands on her shoulders.

"I want you back," he said. "In my show, in my life. We were so good together."

They had never been together. Not like that. Not for his lack of trying. But Lark was not one to lay on her back to get to the top.

"I think what you mean is she's good for you and

your act."

Lark grinned at the heroine coming to her rescue. Spin came up behind Lark and plucked Piers' hands from her shoulders. Then she draped her arm across Lark's shoulder in a clear sign of possession.

"Which really was Lark's act because she was the one who did all the magic," Spin continued.

Lark had no problem letting her friend fight this battle for her. Sure, she could've told Piers off. She had no problem standing up for herself. It was why she was perpetually unemployed.

"I think he probably heard you got a new gig," Spin stage whispered loudly and conspiratorially to Lark. "I'll bet he wants in."

Piers ignored Spin and focused on Lark. "You're a magician's assistant, not a magician. And you're a woman. There aren't many female magicians for a reason. I just want you to succeed."

"Oh, that's so thoughtful of you." Lark left the protection of her best friend's arms and stepped to her former boss. "Stepping in to rescue my show because you don't believe in me."

"That's not what I said."

"I really don't care what you have to say. It would never work," said Lark, her voice thick with mock sadness. "Because in my show I'm in charge, and you clearly don't know what women want."

Piers's features changed in an instant. "But you clearly know what men want. How else did you get Omar al Sharif to give you a show? You're obviously—"

Piers didn't get to finish that sentence. Just as Lark had learned a few magic tricks, she also knew a few defensive maneuvers to put a man in his place. She weaved her hands under Piers's arm and ended with it twisted behind his back. He whimpered in pain like a little boy.

"Um, is there a problem here, my darling?"

Neither Spin nor Lark turned to address Zhi who stood at the far end of the hall.

"Nope," called Spin as she opened the front door. "We've got this, babe."

"All right then. Carry on."

And the two women did just that. They crab-marched the sad excuse for a magician out of the house and slammed the door behind him.

"Men," Lark grumbled as she slumped against the door.

"Most of them," said Spin, looking down the hall. "Not all of them."

Lark had to agree. Most men still only thought of women as objects of pleasure for their needs. Few saw their true worth. The verdict was still out on which camp Omar al Shariff fell into.

CHAPTER FIVE

"Nice shirt. What's it made of? Boyfriend material?"

As pickup lines went, it was inventive. There was the necessary compliment. An ego boost. And even an unexpected double entendre thrown in for good measure.

"If we were out in the street, I'd swear you were the ticket because you are so fine."

The top-heavy, bottle-ginger had curves straight off the racetrack. Looking her up and down made Omar carsick even though he was standing on the parquet floors of his nightclub. He caught the woman's hand before she could fondle the buttons of his shirt.

The Marquis of Navarre was used to this

treatment. Even before becoming a world renowned entertainment producer, women had approached him like he had the checkered pattern of a winning racing flag as a target on his back. When the opposite sex saw him coming, they'd press the pedal with their heels all the way to the metal, not bothering to stay in their own lanes, crashing into one another, and cutting each other off to gain an advantage.

When he was younger, Omar hadn't realized that people were after him for his money and connections. Even though he'd been born into wealth and privilege, he had never learned to take any of it as his due. The blood of his conquering ancestors demanded he create his own empire himself.

So, he did. He assumed everyone else had the same calling. It didn't take too long to realize the fallacy of that belief.

Omar slipped the woman a drink and a dinner voucher and moved on. The fake redhead huffed but slipped the card into her pocket and moved on down the tide. There were a lot of nobles and upper-class crust in his club tonight. The king and soon-to-be-queen were in attendance for one of many parties celebrating their impending nuptials.

Leo and Esme danced close even though the song was upbeat. The monarch's arms were wrapped around his fiancée's torso. Esme's head rested on his chest with her chin tilted up so that Leo could come down for a kiss. With his bride in his arms, Leo looked relaxed. His shoulders were down, and the weight of the kingdom was off his back.

Nearby Alex stood beside his brother. The prince spun Jan around and around until she was an unsteady, giggly thing. Her eyes stayed closed as her world went off kilter. There was complete trust in her posture and movements as though she knew Alex would never let her fall.

DJ Spin was at the turntables mixing in a sick beat. She threw her hands in the air. There was no need for her to tell the crowd to follow suit. They were already worked up into a frenzy. There was only one still body in the crowd.

Zhi leaned against the stage gazing up at the woman he loved as though she were the sun and the moon and the stars rolled in one. Omar was certain the man was hearing wedding bells instead of the pulsing electronic music. Love was definitely in the air around the club.

The spotlight swept across the dance floor,

illuminating newcomers. Omar grimaced and took a step back when he saw his ex prowling into the open doors. Another encounter with Summer was the last thing he wanted.

It was his lucky night. She didn't head in his direction. She veered off course aiming for Daniel.

It was a rare outing for the reclusive bookworm. The Earl of Larida sat off to the side at a table near the exit. He nursed a scotch when he wasn't looking around the room and grimacing at the modern moves and music of today's ton.

Summer slid into the seat next to Daniel. He didn't lift a brow at her presence. Her lips curled and puckered as she spoke to him, close to his ear. Omar could hear her suggested tones from across the crowded room.

She'd had a different tactic when she'd come after Omar. He had fallen for the doe-eyed ingénue act. He'd wanted to not only make Summer a star but to shine as her armored knight.

Daniel wasn't interested in any woman who wasn't on the page. After five minutes of him not uttering a single word or even looking her way, Summer finally dropped the act. She huffed and rose from the table. Dusting off her barely-there cocktail dress, she continued on her prowl.

She must be desperate. The royal wedding was a hot ticket. Every citizen wanted a front row seat to the exclusive invite-only event. Omar was surprised she hadn't finagled an invite with her current boss. Maybe he'd peeped her true colors earlier than Omar had?

Omar ducked out of sight as Summer turned his way. Not that he'd ever get back with her. He was just tired of fighting off unwanted advances for the night. Looking back across the dance floor, he saw that he wasn't the only one disinterested in a partner for the night.

The moment he spotted her, Omar forgot he was being hunted on the most wanted list. As she moved on the dance floor, he moved out of hiding and headed directly into the open arena.

Lark's arms were over her head, fingers splayed in that fan like motion. Her lithe body swayed to the beat in such a way he believed the notes were chasing her and anticipating her moves. Her eyes were closed and her head thrown back as she let the beat catch and carry her away.

He couldn't blame the men eyeing her like hungry wolves. He was doing it too. In fact, he found himself standing a few feet from her not having remembered taking the first step. Unfortunately, another man beat him to the prize.

It was Lord Panek. A scrawny wastrel with deep pockets and enough mistresses to fill an apartment complex. Omar spied a spot of drool at the corner of the man's mouth as he eyed his latest catch. Panek's hands slid towards Lark's waist, but she was gone from the space before his grubby fingers made contact.

Omar watched transfixed as it happened two more times. Lord Romero tried to come up behind her, but she twirled out of his reach. Sir Gottshall aimed for a side approach, mirroring her dance moves. But she did a two-step and shuffled away.

Lark easily evaded all of their advances. And she never once opened her eyes. The woman was magic.

Omar felt he was in a trance just watching her. The sway of her hips, the shimmy of her shoulders, the twirls she performed on light feet. He decided to try his luck at approaching her. Before he could take a step toward her, he was plucked away.

"Why are you hiding?" asked Esme. "Come dance with us."

She pulled him into the circle of his friends. He came willingly because Lark danced on the fringes.

Esme pulled Lark into the circle as well. Lark made no move to evade the future queen.

Esme, Jan, and Lark huddled together. The women moved in time to the fast beat. The three men, the king, the prince, and the marquis, now stood on the fringes watching the women, ensuring no unwanted visitors breached their territory.

The beat changed to a slow song. The couples partnered off, leaving Lark and Omar at the center of the circle. Lark made to step back, but Omar caught her hand. Though he held her, he felt as though he'd been caught.

She didn't come to him immediately. He struggled not to tighten his hold. He wanted her to come willingly. He wanted her to give him the green light.

After the longest second of his life, Lark stepped into his hold. His body sighed into hers, putting itself into Park.

Though he swayed idly on the dance floor, he was raring to go. It had been a long time since he wanted to pursue a woman. Right now he was prepared to throw down his checkered flag and floor it.

"Would you like to be my plus one to the royal wedding?" he asked.

"No, thank you."

The screech of the brakes called him up short. The smell of burnt rubber made him wince. It was the first time he crashed and burned in hot pursuit of the opposite sex.

CHAPTER SIX

It was her own fault.

Lark had easily evaded the unwanted advances of the other men at the party. She'd smelled them each coming a mile away. Entitlement was permanently mixed in their cologne. Their incisors blinded her with the brightness of their misogyny.

Omar walked in those same circles, but somehow, she found herself walking right into the marquis' arms. His big broad arms. He smelled wonderful like always; like fine wine, exotic spices, and a hint of musky, male sweat that only came from a hard day's work.

He held her lightly but securely. His hand wrapped around hers felt strong and capable. She felt the power of him in the tip of his pinky finger, but he didn't force her.

She could've escaped but not without his permission. He gave her a choice. She could run if she chose. The crook of his brow, the question in the lift there instead of a demand, that's what brought her into his loose embrace.

Lark realized too late that she was in a trap. She, a master escape artist, decipherer of illusions, queen of tricks, was caught. And then he dropped the blade down that would slice her in half.

"Would you like to be my plus one to the royal wedding?"

Her answer burst out of her without thought. She'd already sworn never to mix business with pleasure. Even more so not to date the boss.

Omar al Shariff was a real boss. Not a man she needed to prop up like Piers or any other magician she'd worked for. Omar stood tall and proud like the nomadic ancestors of his heritage.

His brow lifted when she declined. He spun her around, and for a moment she worried he might cart her off into his desert kingdom. She worried because she wasn't sure she'd protest her abduction.

Instead of sweeping her off her feet and tossing her over his shoulder, he dipped her. Turning her world upside down. She didn't get dizzy. She kept one foot on the ground.

She expected an argument when he set her to rights. She prepared for an ultimatum. What she got was a delighted grin that brought to mind an amused lion with a wide grin that could swallow her whole.

"You keep surprising me," he said. "I really like that about you."

"Because I don't bow to your wishes?"

She was sure that would wipe the grin off his face. It didn't. It widened.

Omar threw his head back and laughed. The sound was like rolling thunder on a dark night. The kind of night with a fire warming the room and a thick blanket thrown over her legs. Oh, this man was dangerous. If she wasn't careful, he'd pick his way past all her defenses.

"Do you know that an invite to the royal wedding is the one thing everyone in this country wants to get their hands on? Yet you turn it down because you don't want to bow."

"I didn't turn down the invitation," she said. "I turned *you* down."

His brow arched, like an archer readying his weapon.

"I *am* going."

That brow lifted higher, like a bow pulling taught. She couldn't bob and weave to avoid it. She was the only one in its path. Why was she toying with him?

"Going with whom?" His words were clipped and precise. The humming of the M sent a shiver through her.

"With the Duchess of Mondego," she said.

Omar lowered the twin weapons, but Lark stayed on high alert.

"Oh," he said. "I thought one of the scoundrels had snared you."

It was slight, almost imperceptible, but his fingertips curled into the fabric of her dress where he held her at the small of her back.

"I'm not some damsel or princess that needs to be rescued," she said. "If I'm going to star in any story it's going to be as the wizard."

He threw his head back and laughed again. As a counterbalance, he pulled her closer to him.

Bells went off in her head. They weren't alarming. Come to think of it, the sound wasn't exactly a bell. It was more of a gong announcing that something big was commencing. Lark gave her head a shake to silence the reverberations.

"I think we should keep things professional between us," she said.

Omar nodded. His gaze softening but not his hold. "You know whether you said yes or no would not impact my decision to work with you."

Work *with* him. Not *for* him. More than his hold, or his moves on the dance floor, that statement made her heart skip a beat.

"I'm taking a shot on you because I believe in your talent," he continued. "You misunderstood my invitation. I'm the one who needs rescuing."

"You?" said Lark.

"Yes, you see –" Omar began but was interrupted.

"There you are."

Summer breezed in between them, like a stifling wind on a humid day. Her floral scent caught in Lark's throat, making her gag.

"Everyone here is a bore," Summer continued. "Let's hop on your jet for a night in Paris like old times. We'll come back in time for the royal wedding."

Omar sighed looking exhausted. All traces of his laughter and delight gone from his features. His brows looked like broken bows. His hold on Lark firmed like she was his lifeline.

Lark stiffened. That's when he finally let her

loose. She knew he would never hold her against her will. He would never hold anything over her or away from her. If she wanted to, she could lean back in his strong arms, and he'd support her. Just as she could press forward and he'd make way or give her a boost.

Looking Summer up and down, Lark knew the woman had walked all over him. The red stilettos she wore were primed to do it again. Summer wasn't the only one.

Lark looked around the room. She saw past the men who were again sneaking hungry glances at her now that Omar's hold was loosening. Now, she also noticed the gazes of the women.

Omar was trying to avoid the stares and the snares just as she was. And that included Summer. If he let Lark go, they both would be avoiding traps for the rest of the night. That was the reason she gave herself for what she was about to do.

Lark gripped Omar's hand, returning it to the small of her back. Then she snaked her arm around his neck.

Sorry," she said to Summer. "He's taken for the night. And he's also taking me to the wedding."

CHAPTER SEVEN

"Patriarchy is inevitable."

The groans of disapproval, as well as the murmurs of assent, were all deep, gravely, and guttural. Unlike the changing of the times outside these halls, the floor of the Córdovian parliament was decidedly, overwhelmingly male.

"It is a truth you're all ignoring. Male dominance is a biological occurrence."

Lord Panek's voice was a few octaves higher than his colleagues' in the large chamber. To Omar, the middle-aged man sounded like an adolescent boy making threats from behind his nanny's apron strings.

"There is evidence across all ancient and modern

societies, including anthropological evidence."
Panek went on. "Why go against natural law?"

"I'll tell you why," came a feminine voice to the left of Omar. "Because it's the only way you'll ever get a date."

Esme hadn't mastered the art of the stage whisper. Only a few of those in attendance heard the soon-to-be-queen's remarks. What turned heads were the snorts and snickers coming from Omar and Zhi who sat beside her. The marquis and duke covered their mouths in a belated attempt to stifle their amusement.

Over the years, women had increased in the halls of the Córdovian Parliament. But the female species were only mere dots of dim light in the actual seats on the dark, masculine landscape. Yet, the truth was that most estates and businesses across the nation were run by those of the female persuasion.

Omar's older sister, Alana, ran the marquisette back in the coastal province of Navarre. The seat of Navarre once guarded the southeastern coastlines of Córdoba. They still had a fleet. Only now it was of ships that brought in spices and goods from the Middle East and Northern Africa.

Just as he'd happily handed the reins of the estate over to her, he wanted to finally vacate his seat in the House of Lords as well and let her take the pedestal. Alana loved running the lands and moving the pieces in the game of politics.

Omar always lost to her in the game of Battleship, where his ships were perpetually sunk. He was bored watching these proceedings. His mind often drifted to wondering if he could make the parliamentary proceedings into a musical. But the thought of lords arguing the rights of women left a distasteful tang in his mouth.

"The British monarchy has changed the law of succession," chimed in King Leonidas. "Does Córdoba truly want to remain behind the Windsors?"

A light rumble went through the crowd, lightening the mood. Lord Panek and his lackeys sneered at the king.

Pretty soon, the back and forth died down. It was time to get to business. King Leo rose from his seat. It was rare for a monarch to have a seat at the table, but Leo had never been much of a figurehead. He was a man of action.

"It's time to vote," he said.

One by one, the members came forward to cast

their votes. The outcome wasn't a surprise. The margins, however, were. The measure passed by a one to ninety margin. Apparently, even Lord Panek's lackeys didn't want to stand with him. In every way, women were now equal to the men in all classes and positions of power in Córdoba.

Esme leaped out of her seat and into Leo's arms with the announcement. Another perk of the law changing was the abolition of the noble blood clause, where royals could only marry partners of a blue bloodline. It was just in time as their wedding was this weekend.

Leo embraced his bride in a royal display of affection that the members of the governing body had never seen in its hallowed halls. They would all need to get used to it; having hugs as part of the curriculum with an American kindergarten teacher on the throne.

In addition to the school teacher being in the line of succession, an American pie maker was now fifth in line for the crown. If Omar was a conspiracy theorist, he'd say there was a low key invasion on the front. Even the Duke of Mondego was head over heels in love with a woman with Yankee blood.

"So, you and Lark?" said Zhi.

Omar didn't allow his head to swivel and do a

double take at the duke's words. He kept his features impassive and his gaze forward. "There is no me and Lark."

For that statement to be true, his heart shouldn't be skipping beats when their names were placed side by side in the same sentence.

"Riiiight," Zhi drawled the single word, letting it stretch into the truth of Omar's statement. "Male nobles are getting caught like flies being drawn to an American apple pie."

"Lark isn't American."

"Her mother is an ex-patriot."

Now he did do a double take. Omar didn't know that about her. He felt an intense pang of jealousy that Zhi knew something about Lark that he didn't.

"I can't wait to see who snares the Earl," Zhi continued.

That notion was ridiculous; the idea of the Earl of Larida dating anyone outside of his library. Daniel rarely looked up from a book long enough to eat, let alone notice the opposite sex. But Omar and Lark?

There it went again. The placement of their names side by side made his heart skip two beats this time.

Omar couldn't deny that he was attracted to her.

He didn't admit it to Zhi either. Omar was now a looker and not a toucher.

Though the idea of his hands on the shapely magician ...

Omar looked over to see Zhi grinning at him, a knowing glint in his gaze.

"It's just a business thing." Omar patted at the breast pocket of his three-piece suit. It was empty, of course. But he couldn't shake the feeling he'd misplaced something.

"You have a reputation for *things* with your female business associates," said Zhi.

"You know that's not true." Omar turned to see the duke's light eyes narrowed in a dark glare. His hands fell away from the empty pockets at his chest and rested in his lap.

"I'm glad you admit it," said Zhi. "Don't make me have to pull out the dueling swords."

"You'd fight for her honor?"

"Oh no," Zhi raised his brows. "Not me. Spin."

Omar shuddered, the hair on the nape of his neck stiffened at the thought. When he'd first met the DJ, he'd been certain she could cut a man with that silent glare. When he'd seen DJ Spin perform, spinning disks, he often got the impression that she could easily transform into a ninja wielding vinyl throwing stars. He decided it was best to turn the tables on this conversation.

"Have you popped the question to the delectable DJ yet?" he asked.

Zhi leaned back in his seat, appearing entirely at ease with the direction of the new topic. "Not yet. Not during this circus, anyway. Spin deserves her own spotlight."

They both gazed over at the happy couple. Cameras flashed as the royal couple held up the signed bill. Esme turned to Leo and gave him a peck on the cheek. The small sign of affection was innocent, but it wasn't the normal protocol. The press ate it up, and the bulbs went off like fireworks.

Omar was happy for his oldest friend. But he was also happy to have the spotlight off of him. Since Leo's engagement, followed by the prince's engagement, the cameras had blessedly been out of his face and his dating life. It was a rare breath of fresh air.

"So," Zhi continued. "Don't go proposing to Lark first."

It took a moment for Omar to get his tongue to work. "I'm not proposing to her. I'm not even dating her."

"I've seen the way you look at her."

Wow, was he that obvious? From the first hour that they'd spent together driving from the docks to House Mondego, Omar had tried not to stare. Apparently, he'd failed. Lark had captivated him from her sleight of hand to her infectious smile.

"I've also seen the way she looks at you."

That perked Omar up. "She's been looking at me?"

Zhi turned a sly glance on Omar. If there had been any doubt before, the duke had his confirmation now.

It didn't matter. There wouldn't be anything between Omar and Lark. Except for one outing to the royal wedding. That was an arrangement of convenience, not a date. It was made only to get the sharks off both their backs.

Omar was Lark's boss. She was his employee. Neither wanted to go down the road of that tired trope.

Lark had real talent. She didn't need gossip sheets to give her career a boost. And Omar definitely didn't need to be featured in another spread.

CHAPTER EIGHT

"Oof." Lark landed with a thud on the mattress beneath the stage's trap door.

"Hey, where did she go?" call Blaze from above. "It's so hard to find good help these days."

Lark could vouch for that. Blaze had designs on being a magician someday, the star of his own show with his own magician's assistant. Luckily, the kid had the chops … to be a magician. He was sorely lacking in the assistant division, which was his current area of employment.

Blaze had the stage presence and theatricality necessary for a showman. But he lacked the magical technique and attention to detail necessary in an assistant's role.

The mattress she would disappear on was a few

inches off center of its mark. It wasn't enough to cause her injury. Not in this trick. But inches added up.

"We need to run that trick one more time," said Lark when she came back on stage.

Blaze startled as she came upon him. It wasn't from the place she was supposed to reappear to complete the trick.

"Why?" he asked. "The disappearing act trick is in the bag."

The kid was young. But luckily the youth was malleable. He was learning what was traditionally women's work in the magic world. It was way harder than it appeared.

"You're doing great on the misdirection and leading the attention away," Lark said in a gentle tone of correction. "It's the ditch, the disposal of the object—namely, me—that is a little wonky. We need to practice the trick until it's second hat. We need to nail this preview."

Omar had set up a preview with some of Europe's biggest movers and shakers. In just a matter of days, they'd fill the seats of the theater. Their reception would impact the future of her show. Though she knew Omar had her backing financially, it was all in with the components of the show as she envisioned them, she needed more than an audience of one. Even if the idea of entertaining Mr. Tall, Dark, and Handsome one-on-one had its appeal.

"The marquise is all in with this show," said Blaze. "Especially now that you're seeing him."

Lark's head did a one-hundred eighty-degree turn, like in a horror movie. "I'm not seeing Mr. al Shariff."

"No? He's taking you to the royal wedding."

"It's not a date. It's business."

Lark busied herself resetting the setup for the trick herself. The last thing she wanted to do was put her life in the hands of a man again. Perhaps she could do this show on her own without any assistance?

Blaze moved toward her. His hands were up like he was showing her that they were empty, and no trick was in play. "Look, I'm not judging. The world isn't fair. I know what women have to go through to get an advantage in this day and age."

"You do?" Lark cocked a hand on her hip. Her hands were not empty. If the wrong word came out of his mouth, she'd make a pink slip appear.

Omar was the boss of her. But she was the boss

of her assistant. He was replaceable. He should know that.

"That fine dance of flirting some women have to do without giving up the goods. I've seen it all too many times."

For a man who missed the finer points of his job, he sure got the major points of today's society. At least how things were in the entertainment industry where many predators were loose.

"I haven't given up any goods," said Lark.

"Then you're not as smart as I thought you were," said a sultry female voice.

Lark turned to look into the dark of the theater. Summer moved in and out of the overhead lights. Dark then light, like a star falling from the sky on a cloudy night. The dying light was obscured by the pressing fog.

"I was once in your shoes," she continued. "On that same stage as you. In that very same spotlight, in fact."

"Did you notice they change the billing outside?" said Lark.

"Sassy. He likes sass. He likes shiny. You're a shiny new toy. But you'll dull soon, and he'll get bored and toss you over."

Lark's instinct was to say that that wasn't the

Omar she knew. He'd never shown her that side. But what did she know?

She'd heard about his reputation for dating the women he produced. She'd also heard his side of the story. She wanted to believe him. But was that because she wanted to dance with him more?

"It's his M. O.," Summer continued. "He always dates his starlets, especially if he thinks they'll go far. I think he lives vicariously since he doesn't have any talent of his own."

"I suppose that's why he passed you over."

"Cute."

"Sassy and cute. Clearly, I'm on my way up."

One thing Lark was sure of was that she wouldn't let this has-been wannabe intimidate her.

"You're headed up," said Summer. "Until you're on your way down. Stars don't last forever. They're bright balls of fire. Sooner or later, you'll run out of fuel. Best to have a backup plan. Consider Rancik Entertainment. He doesn't make stars, he makes careers."

Summer placed a business card on the edge of the stage, right over the trap door for the disappearing act. After the woman made her way out of the exit, Lark pulled the lever, and the card fluttered down, landing to the side of the mattress below.

"I'll go line that up," said Blaze, peering down at the card.

"No," said Lark. "It's exactly where it needs to be."

"Don't forget you have lunch with the executives from Vizier Bank about purchasing the new theater," said Marlena. "You also have lunch scheduled with the Prime Minister."

Omar tried and failed to stifle a sigh. He genuinely liked the Prime Minister. The working class man was just a few years younger than him and a good number of steps down the social class ladder. But he'd bootstrapped his way up the golden stair for a seat at the noble table.

"You also need to take a look at these contracts for the summer concert series. One of the boy bands isn't happy with the rider."

Omar looked down at his planner. His time was blocked from the time he woke up until he laid his head on the pillow at night. He hadn't gotten into this line of work to be bound to a desk and schedule. He became a producer to have a hand in creating and spreading art, music, color, and movement to the world.

Looking down at the pile of documents cluttering his desk, he saw a flash of color. A woman leaped into a man's arms in the still image. The Balletto di Roma had a new show opening tonight. On his desk was an invitation. Omar loved all forms of entertainment, including watching men in tights throw girls up into the air.

He felt not a pinprick of an attack on his masculinity for that. In fact, he wished he could see it in person. But his schedule held him tight to his desk.

Marlena laid more files down on top of the mounting piles on his desk. Banks, politicians, legalese; none of these were the reason Omar had walked away from a marquisate. His pleading gaze went to his longtime assistant.

Marlena was of average height, not too short, not exactly tall. She couldn't be called thin, but neither was she overweight. She had the average figure of a Córdovian woman. Her hair was light brown that could some days pass for honey blonde as often as it could be called plain brown. Her features were lined with age, but there weren't as many lines as the years of her actual age. However old that might be. Omar had never bothered to find out. What mattered to him was that she kept him on top of things and got unwanted distractions, namely women, off of him.

"By the way," said Marlena. "Your old flame was here earlier."

Omar huffed like a child being forced to eat his Brussels sprouts. He'd rather deal with the boy band's demands than face off with Summer. Marlena waved her hand like moving the dish aside.

"I sent her away," said Marlena. "But the new girl wants a word."

"New girl?" asked Omar. "Do you mean Lark?"

Marlena shrugged. "I don't bother remembering their names until their name is in lights."

"Her name is in lights on the marquee of the Main Street Theater."

Marlena didn't look at him. She ticked off items on her clipboard. "Should I send her away too?"

"No."

Marlena wrinkled her nose like there was a new batch of tiny cabbages on her clipboard.

"Fine, I'll send her in. But you do have a lot of

work to get to before you spend the rest of your day playing with the help."

Marlena had been with Omar since the beginning. In the beginning, he had played much harder than he'd worked. Dashing off to New York for a play or to London for a concert or Moscow for the ballet. But the work always got done because he loved his job.

Marlena loved her job too. His office was the ultimate velvet rope, and his assistant took pleasure in keeping people out. Omar had always suspected that Marlena would've made a great casting director; telling more people no than yes. But in spite of the opportunities that were present for her, she'd stuck by his side. For that, he allowed her to mouth off from time to time.

"There's nothing going on between myself and Ms. Voorheen."

"Of course not, sir. I'll show her in, and then you can get on with your *nothing*."

Her words were efficient as ever but insincere. Omar didn't offer a retort because when Marlena opened the door, Lark stood on the other side. Omar rose like the moth he was to her flame. There wasn't any light shining on her. It was coming from within her.

She wore thin straps that showed off the heart shape of her collarbones. Her arms were tan and toned in the green dress. Her skin shone as though she'd bloomed from the earth. The fabric of her skirt swished around her long legs as though playing at her calves. Omar wanted to join in the fun.

"I changed my mind," Lark said when the door closed behind her.

"That's fine." He was prepared to agree with anything she said, give her anything she wanted.

She was a fairy nymph standing before him. He had the urge to eat something from her hands. That's how the fae trapped humans, wasn't it? His stomach grumbled as he stepped closer.

"I can't go with you to the royal wedding."

He'd give her anything, except that.

"I don't want there to be any perception that we're dating," she said. "I don't want anyone to think I got to the top on my back. Because I am going to the top. I have every intention of climbing the ladder on my feet."

Omar didn't want that either. What he wanted was to carry her up the ladder. Not because she needed him to. He wanted to be of service to this amazing woman. He wanted to be by her side when she went places. Because she was right; she was going places. And one of those places would be to the royal wedding with him so that every man in Córdoba, every man in the world, would know that he, Omar al Shariff, the Marquis of Navarre was her champion.

But he had to know, "What brought this on, Lark?"

"I had a run-in with your ex."

Summer? Marlena had said she'd sent her away today. But it looked like Summer had gotten to his current talent before that.

"The truth is, you don't need me," he said.

Lark's eyes went wide. Her lips shaped into a perfect O that he ached to taste. What stopped him was the flash of vulnerability that tinted the corners of her eyes.

"You would've made it on your own," he continued. "People are going to see that the moment you step onto the stage. I'd like to remain a part of your journey, if only just to watch your star rise. But if you think someone can launch you better ... If there's someone else you'd rather work with ..."

They were words. He meant most of them. The part about her talent and that she could've made it on her own. But he had no intention of letting her go. Not professionally. He was fighting a losing battle of grabbing hold of her romantically.

Lark closed her eyes and breathed a weary sigh. When she refocused on him, Omar let out his own sigh of relief. Whether it be his words or something else, he knew she wasn't going anywhere. They were in this together.

"I'm sorry," she said. "I don't want to leave you. No one's ever seen my vision so clearly as you. Or has given me so much freedom to bring it alive. I've never had this before."

There were just two steps between them. He took one. "I haven't worked with someone as talented as you in a long time. Someone I don't have to actually tinker with because the magic is already there."

He took the last remaining step. The ceiling fan lifted the scent from her shoulders and brought it to his nose. Omar swallowed down the sweet nectar of Lark, and he knew the legends about fairies and food were true. He was now her captive.

But the joke was on him. She'd captured him, but she had no interest in keeping him.

It was a novel experience. A woman wanting to keep her distance from him on a personal level to protect her career.

Lark stepped out of his path. She turned, so they were both facing the closed door to his office. Standing beside him, her shoulder almost brushed his. The half an inch of air between them pulsed with potent energy; like two magnets pulling them together. Only he wasn't sure that she felt it too.

"Looks like you're stuck with me then," she said. "I really appreciate how professional you've been in all our encounters. By now, the man in power would have already tried to maul me. But not you."

"Nope. Not me."

"You're one of a kind."

"Yup. That's me."

"It's not easy being a woman in show business."

"It's not easy being a man in power either."

Lark quirked one of those perfectly arched brows at him. Her mouth twisted in a wry smile. Omar had to grip the edges of his desk not to launch himself at her and maul her like the beast he truly was.

"Not to pull out the world's tiniest violin," he said, "but it ain't easy being me. Women and men chase me all the time for what I can do for them. I never know who's genuinely interested."

"I understand that." Her voice lowered in a tone

of mock conspiracy. "I was a hot commodity in the magician's community. I know all the tricks."

"I got that impression by your act." Omar grinned, flashing his teeth. He had to press his lips together to keep from taking a bite.

Perhaps she sensed the danger because her grin slipped. "I just don't want people looking down on me."

"Honestly, there's nothing you can do to control that."

"I beg to differ. I'm an illusionist."

Omar chuckled but quickly sobered when an idea flashed in his mind. "I want you to come somewhere with me."

"Not a date." Her shoulders gave a shake, like her feathers, or rather wings were ruffled.

"Not a date," he agreed. "A break. I need one, and I'm taking you with me. You game?"

CHAPTER TEN

*A*fter storming into her boss' office, Lark didn't know what possessed her to take Omar's arm and go on an adventure into the unknown. It was exactly the opposite goal she'd had going in there.

As they walked out of his office door, she felt the eyes on her. His assistant shot her daggers as Omar canceled his entire day to spend it with her. But Lark couldn't hold tight to any embarrassment or shame at stepping out with her employer in the middle of the workday. The farther they got from his office, the more the tension seeped off his broad shoulders, out of his muscled forearms, and out the long fingertips that grazed her skin.

It was as though the businessman had been a

mirage, and the new man was emerging. It fascinated her to watch the transformation. But she couldn't escape the judgment of the gazes that tracked them to the elevator.

Phone conversations paused. Chatter at the water cooler died down. Typing halted.

It continued outside the building. People stared on the streets as he handed her into his town car. She caught the driver's passionless gaze as she slipped into the back seat. As they sped through the high street of the capital, Lark was certain the blurry faces going by were all taking a hard, long gander at her behind the tinted glass of the luxury car.

"This is probably a mistake," she said.

She turned to Omar, expecting him to pounce now that he had her exactly where he wanted her. Omar didn't leap on her. He sat across from her on the opposite side of the car. He crossed one ankle over his knee and shut his eyes. Even then, with plenty of space, he didn't man spread his long legs.

After a moment, he opened his eyes and leaned forward. But it was to ask her one and then another question. "So, you're half American?"

"I ... uh, yes."

"I didn't know that about you. Tell me more." He

leaned back, gaze on her, and waited patiently for her to begin her life story.

And so she did. She told him about growing up in the theater with her American mother who was once on a chorus line, and her French father who worked backstage. All of Lark's siblings were in the business. Her older brother was a set designer. Her younger sister was a property mistress. Lark was the only performer.

At some point, Omar leaned forward again. But it was to ask a follow-up question about her mother's time on Broadway. Then another question about the companies her father worked for. Then a few questions about her siblings' work.

It kept going like that all through the drive; Omar asking her questions and showing genuine interest in her answers. Being a good conversationalist, Lark didn't let the chat remain one-sided.

She asked after him and learned that he was the youngest of two. That came as a surprise. With such a commanding presence and personality, she'd assumed he was the oldest and only child. His smile was broad and bright as he told Lark about his tyrant, older sister and how she'd nearly tripled the value of the empire their ancestors had built.

Lark came to a jolt when the car stopped. She'd forgotten they were in a moving vehicle. She'd forgotten to worry about who'd been watching them. Looking out the window, she saw that there was no one around. They'd stopped at a private airfield.

"When you said a break, I didn't think you meant the sound barrier."

Omar flashed those white teeth at her. For the second time today, she felt he could surely take a bite out of her. But she didn't fear for her life. She feared for her loss of self-preservation.

"Backing out?" he asked.

"No," she squared her jaw. "Just wondering if I need a passport?"

He shrugged. "One of the Italian officials at the gate owes me a favor."

"Italy?" Her jaw dropped. "I can't go to Italy. I have a show to prepare for."

"You were born ready. Besides, I know your boss. He's pretty cool about this kind of thing."

Omar opened the door and climbed out. He turned back to her and held out his hand.

Lark hesitated. "I have to tell Spin."

Omar pulled out his phone and tapped a few

keys. "I just told Zhi. And I'll have you back by your curfew."

"I don't have a curfew. I'm a grown woman."

"Yes." He flashed those teeth again. His voice, when he spoke, was the low rumble of a tiger. "I know you are."

His hand had remained extended the entire time. After one more second, Lark took it. When his skin met hers, she willed the butterflies in her belly to stop fluttering.

They were no match for this predator. If he was hunting for her, which he wasn't, she would not be easy prey. Even with that assertion, the fluttering didn't stop. It increased.

"Can I ask where we're going?"

"Via del Corso."

Lark's feet tripped over themselves, but Omar caught her and brought her to rights.

"The Corso?" she breathed. "That's the Rodeo Drive of Rome."

"Well, you're not properly attired for our plans."

"Are you trying to *Pretty Woman* me?"

He laughed. "I'll be Richard Gere-ing myself as well. I need a tux for where we're going. A simple suit and tie won't cut it at Teatro Sistina."

"The Sistina? Isn't the Balletto di Roma in residence there?"

"Oh, good. I don't have to twist your arm."

Lark tried to swallow down her incredulity. It wouldn't pass her throat. So, she let it out. "I can't believe I get to go. I've always wanted to see them."

"It's opening night, and I have tickets." Omar held up a golden envelope.

"Are you trying to impress me?"

"Honestly, no. I'm trying to relax, and I'd like to do that with you. Because I don't have to work hard with you."

Lark stopped arguing. Instead of fighting or trying to find a reason to flee, she climbed the steps to the private plane. She strapped in and settled in for the adventure.

Two hours later she walked out of a couture shop in an exquisite ball gown of midnight blue with silver sparkles. She looked and felt like magic.

Stepping over the threshold of the shop, she heard a purring sound off to the side. She turned to find Omar in a tux. The next low rumble of appreciation came from her throat.

Lark was playing with fire and not the fake flames from a magic shop. She'd felt the spark between them. At some point while crossing the sea, that spark had caught.

Inside the private box of the theater, the blaze grew cozy as they both leaned forward when the dancers leaped and twirled onto the stage. At some point during the second act, their hands found their way to each other. She wasn't sure who'd reached for whose first. It may have been mutual.

In any case, the flame had ignited to something she could no longer control. It was so bright that Lark was sure everyone in the theater could see it. But no one turned to them as the house lights came on announcing the end of the performance.

"You're right," he said, as they sat in the emptying theater.

"Of course, I am," she said. "About what?"

"If we dated it would reflect badly on both our careers."

"Oh."

Lark's chin lowered to her chest. His fingers went limp. But he didn't loosen his grip. His palm tightened around her hand.

"I'd be labeled a predator and would never get another true talent. Bad press and tabloids would outshine your talent."

"Yeah." Her breath caught in the uncertainty of where he was going with this.

"So, we both know what has to be done."

Omar turned to her. Those broad shoulders boxed her into the private alcove of their seats. His dark gaze was as sharp as throwing daggers. His eyes pinned her to the back of her chair.

"We lie about us," he said.

"Us?"

"Get rid of the question mark, Lark. We both know that there is an us."

He was right. She was past hesitating. A glimmer of certainty rose through the flame that encased them. Lark gave him a single nod. Like the caged tiger she'd always expected him to be, he pounced.

His mouth covered hers. Not soft. Not sweet. His kiss had a bite to it.

She felt consumed by the touch of his mouth on hers. The pads of his fingers were soft, but they still clawed into her chin, into her shoulders, into her low back.

Lark forgot to care if anyone saw. She was caught. She was claimed. She had no plans to escape anytime soon.

CHAPTER ELEVEN

For the first time in a long time, Omar bounced out of bed in the morning. His alarm clock startled him twenty minutes later after he'd already finished dressing. He was out of the door just as the sun was stretching its rays into the new day.

That single kiss from Lark had breathed new life into him like she'd cast magic into his veins with the press of her lips.

Oh, that first kiss.

Omar was a man used to fine wine and fine dining. Lark Voorheen's lush lips were a singular delicacy. It had taken everything in him not to gorge himself on the nectar that was her top lip.

He'd felt sated simply with her presence, talking

to her on the car ride, learning more about her family and past on the plane ride, sharing in her delight at the ballet.

But when the curtain went down, he could no longer believe the lie. It wasn't enough. He needed more than a seat at the table beside her.

He itched to do more than having her back while she went after her dreams. Omar wanted to be a part of her dreams, as she had been a part of his since the first night he'd met her.

That first kiss had been a dream come true.

The second kiss, in the car ride to the airfield, surpassed his waking fantasies.

He'd taken another kiss when he'd left her at the front door of Mondego House.

When he lingered, pressing kisses to her temple, the lights had flickered off and on. Omar caught Zhi scowling at him from the window. Spin stood in front of the duke, holding two thumbs up at her best friend.

Lark had slipped inside, leaving Omar only with the vivid memories of embracing her which had turned his once-fevered dreams into mirages last night.

Seeing her standing backstage that morning, she looked like a fairy standing in the sunlight. The woman positively shimmered. Omar was afraid to approach her in fear she'd disappear.

But as he came closer, she didn't vanish. She lifted her gaze, and their eyes locked. His eyes weren't playing tricks on him, she was glowing. It wasn't the shimmering lotion he knew stage performers wore. It was all her.

The corners of her mouth tilted up, and somehow he was standing before her. Their lips parted at the same moment, but no words came. A tingling touched the tip of every one of Omar's fingertips, as though he had ten wands ready to capture the magic of her. She was nearly in his arms, but she strong-armed him.

Instead of the vibrant woman before him, his hands closed around empty air. The sensation was like a tiny explosion going off in his palms. He felt burned by the rejection.

Omar couldn't fathom what he'd done wrong since last they'd met?

"We have a crowded house," she said.

He peered out of the curtain. There were at least a dozen reporters gathered in the front rows. He cursed under his breath.

He'd forgotten about the press junket. Now that Lark's show was ready, it was time for him to hold up his end of the bargain and get the word out. This Q&A, followed by a brief demonstration, was the first of his planned promotional campaign. There would also be television and radio ads, a social media blitz, and he was in talks to do some merchandising with wands, t-shirts, and some simple magic kits.

Lark was already a star in his eyes. He was about to make her a brand. First, he had to deal with these nosy reporters. They'd be looking for any signs of a relationship between him and his new protégé. Omar had no intention of letting them in on this relationship. This one he wanted to keep all to himself.

It would be no hardship pretending he was disinterested now. He was in a foul mood. The woman he wanted was right in front of him and out of his reach.

"Let's get this over with," he growled. "And then I can sweep you off your feet where you belong."

"Caveman," she said.

He took a step toward her, invading her space like it was his due.

Lark held her ground.

"Cavemen were sheltered wimps hiding inside

rocks," Omar scoffed. "My people conquered the deserts."

"You think I'll fall into the stereotype of a white, western woman who's set up to tame the barbaric, alpha-hole sultan?" She arched that mocking eyebrow that set him aflame with desire.

"You think I can be tamed?" He wiggled an amused eyebrow of his own.

Her lips twitched. Whether from amusement or desire, he was determined to find out.

A throat cleared off to the side of the stage. Marlena stood with her clipboard raised. Both of her brows were narrowed in disappointed slits. Her tone, when she spoke, was clipped. "We have a schedule to keep."

Omar let out a haggard sigh. He stepped back from Lark with great reluctance and opened the curtain. For now, he'd share her with the world. But later, an abduction would be taking place with a certain magical woman.

He had plans for that evening. He'd take her to the Prince's Pallet. They could go in the back and sit in the private room. He wanted to wine and dine her, soften her up with sweet treats. Then he'd take her back to his place ... and show her a performance tape from a show he was considering.

More than anything, he wanted Lark's opinion. He couldn't wait to hear what she thought of the dance troupe. And then, once he knew her thoughts, he'd kiss her senseless.

But first, they had to earn the good opinion of the entertainment reporters and critics. They walked out to the flashing of bulbs and shouts. The press didn't wait for Omar's prepared remarks. They asked the burning question.

"Any truth to the rumor about you two dating?"

"Ms. Voorheen and I have a working relationship," Omar started, the lie rolling smoothly off the tongue that had tasted Lark's sweetness. "I have great respect for her unique talent and am excited to present it to the world."

"The two of you were seen in Rome last night."

"Business trip," said Omar.

"We understand she'll be your date to the royal wedding this weekend."

"No," said Lark.

All eyes, microphones, and pens turned to her.

"I'll be the Duchess of Mondego's date to the wedding."

Pens stopped waggling. Cameras shuttered dark. Mouths gaped askew.

"So, you and the Duchess are ...?"

"Living together," Lark finished the sentence for the reporter.

In an instant, the flashes started up again. The pens scribbled furiously. A barrage of questions left the reporters' mouths at this scandalous bit of news. Lark turned and whispered to Omar.

"First rule of magic? Distraction. It works every time."

She winked and then walked center stage to show them the vanishing trick she'd prepared. More than anything, Omar wanted this particular show and tell over so they could pull a disappearing act of their own.

CHAPTER TWELVE

"Ever wish someone would disappear into thin air?" Lark asked, her gaze slid to the overzealous reporter who'd badgered her and Omar with questions about their personal lives and not the show.

The rest of the peanut gallery chuckled, having caught her side eye. Clearly, that particular reporter wasn't well liked by his peers. Lark was excellent at getting people to like and trust her.

"I'm going to let you all in on the trick," she continued.

The crowd of reporters put down their pens and leaned forward. Cameras lowered so that eyes could get better views of the action.

"The trick is, you can't control other people, only yourself."

Many gazes narrowed in suspicion. Good. A good trick required a few skeptics. Those were the ones who'd be too busy trying to figure out how the trick was done. What they didn't realize was that by following her every motion, she still had them in the palm of her hand because she was still the one leading them around.

There was a dance to magic; a partner dance. It required one party to lead and the other to follow. The trick was in getting the audience to believe they were in control.

The press was easily led to believe they knew what was going on. They trusted Lark as she set them up. It was easy. Everyone wanted to believe the illusion.

"You'll need a large sheet, some sequins, and a handful of glitter." Lark Vanna White'd her props, spreading her arms wide to encompass the table of items sitting on a blood red wing backed chair at the center of the stage. "The crafts are to make things pretty. People are distracted by beautiful things."

"You can say that again," came a murmur just off stage.

The Marquis of Navarre was not so easily

diverted. Omar's gaze was locked on her every move. It was proving impossible to hide everything from him. With each glance, with each caress, Lark didn't want to play any tricks with this man.

He had that glassy look of a man mesmerized. Even though she clearly dazzled him, the intelligence in his gaze told her he wasn't fooled.

Worse, the heat in his gaze was going to ruin the illusion of them not dating. If the press took a good hard look between the two of them, they'd see right through it all. With a snap of her wrists, Lark unfurled the sparkly blanket and brought all the attention back to herself.

"The next step in the trick is to ask for a volunteer. But that person should be in on the trick."

Lark crooked a finger at the meddlesome reporter. The man hesitated. But then his gaze sparkled with opportunity.

"You're going to hold the blanket high," she said to the reporter, handing him the prop. "When I say the magic words, you'll let it fall. Meanwhile, I'll throw up some glitter to distract our audience. Then I'll duck behind this wingback chair that I've inconspicuously put here."

"That's it?" asked the reporter, seemingly completely unimpressed.

"Yup." Lark nodded. "Do you think you can handle it?"

He snorted.

Lark turned slightly and winked at the audience. The reporters still in their chairs grinned back realizing another trick was afoot.

The reporter-assistant held up the blanket. "Abracadabra," he said. Only he dropped the blanket before the entire word was out of his mouth.

The crowd gasped. Pencils rolled off their laps as a few got to their seats. Lark wasn't there.

The reporter assistant peeked behind the wingback chair. A small puff of air blew his hair back. When he straightened, the crowd of reporters fell back into their seats laughing hysterically.

"She glitter-bombed him!"

"Wait, where did she go?"

"I don't know, but I can't wait to see the whole show."

One person hadn't been fooled by Lark's misdirection. That man turned from the stage to look at the exit of the trap door. Omar had seen her coming a mile away.

In the darkness of the theater's backstage, Lark slipped out of the spotlight and into his arms. Using another secret door, he swept her from the stage and up to his office floor. He misdirected the calls for his attention from his assistant and staff. Then he filled his palms with her and pressed his mouth to hers.

Omar al Shariff made her knees feel rooted with his light touches. He fed her hunger with his seeking kisses. Here was a man who respected her talent. He listened to her ideas. He also set her blood on fire with his cool glances.

"You were magnificent out there," he said between kisses. "I underestimated your talent."

Lark preened under his praise. It wasn't the first time a man had complimented her. It usually came with a follow-up request that she do something to benefit him.

"You're going to be more than a hit. You're going to be a rocket ship. Starship. There's just one thing I need you to do for me."

Lark bit her lip on the same spot he'd just nibbled. Her chest urged her to release the breath she was holding. But her lungs wouldn't let go.

"Will you call the Duchess and warn her about the publication of your salacious relationship? Otherwise, Zhi will have my head."

The long-held breath came out in a gush. Then a giggle. Then a snort.

Omar's dark gaze glittered with amusement

watching her cover her mouth and the embarrassing noises coming from them. When she went silent, he pulled her back to him. "I don't know how I'm going to keep my distance from you at the wedding?"

"It'll be easy. Women will be flocking to you."

"What women? They all pale to your sparkle."

"Smooth." Lark patted his chest, getting distracted by the corded muscle she found there.

"Truth," he said. "I want to see you tonight."

"We can't leave out together. They'll know."

"Fine," he sighed.

That was too easy. Lark got the feeling this fight was far from over. She saw she was right when Omar handed her a card.

"Meet me here," he said. "Dress comfortably. It's going to be a long night."

He kissed her again. Her lips were swollen by the time he reluctantly released her.

She wobbled like her feet left the ground. She'd never been swept off her feet by a man a day in her life. Who knew that all that would take was a man who simply believed in her and gave her a boost up the ladder of success.

CHAPTER THIRTEEN

"Are we going back to Italy?" asked Lark as they pulled up to the private airfield that housed his company jet.

"Not so far this time," Omar said.

It was hard to move words past his throat. His tongue was either salivating or tied in knots around this woman.

Just looking at her and he was lost. Even now, she wore a simple dress. Strappy heels and a shimmering wrap. He'd seen women in expensive gowns whose fabric could feed a small country. Not one looked as stunning as she did in the simple gown she'd likely gotten from a department store.

"If not Italy, then where?" she asked.

"You'll see when we get there."

"So, you're kidnapping me? Regressing back to your ancient ways?"

"Kidnapping means one party is unwilling." He held out his hand to her. As he opened his palm, he felt he was baring his soul. "Do you trust me?"

Her breath caught. Her nostrils flared. She didn't say the words, but it was right there in her eyes.

She did trust him. The revelation of the fact appeared to surprise her. It surprised him too.

Her fingertips sliding into his hand left trails of fire, like a comet's tail. Her palm meeting his was a supernova. Omar's universe broke apart and reformed. The new center of his galaxy was this woman who'd come into his orbit.

Bypassing the jet, Omar handed his precious cargo into the helicopter. Even though she came with him of her own free will, he strapped her into the safety harness himself, pulling the belt tight so she couldn't escape.

Lark made not one complaint. Not one single demand. She was like no woman he'd ever dated.

The *whoop whoop* of the helicopter blades matched the pounding of his own heart. He was already feeling lightheaded before the lift-off.

Once in the air, every time Lark's gaze went wide, he leaned forward. He needed to know why.

So he could buy, capture, or create whatever sight had pleased her.

"It's beautiful," she breathed.

Omar looked out the window. The crystal blue in the Córdovian skyline was before them. He flew a lot, but he rarely took the time to take in the scenery when up high.

The golden spires glistened in the setting sun. There was ancient architecture set between modern skyscrapers. Above, stars lit up the night sky as though a parent had switched off a child's overhead light and turned on their nightlight. They twinkled in her eyes. Omar made a mental note to travel by air at night as often as possible if it pleased her.

Thirty minutes later, Lark's gaze went even wider with awe and delight. Omar had scarcely taken his gaze off her for the duration of the copter ride. He saw a familiar setting in her pale eyes. A medieval castle with domes instead of spires reflected back from Lark's depths.

"Where are we?" Lark asked.

"Home," he said.

Once the bird touched down on the roof of the Navarre Castle, Omar sprang from his seat. He brushed Lark's hands away from the release catch and performed the honor himself. If she was going to get away, it would be directly into his arms.

"This is your castle?" she asked once she was free and caught in his arms.

"Yes," he said. "Well, it was. I gave it up. My sister runs the place. I still have the title for now, but she has all the power."

"You just handed over your power to a woman?"

"Running a marquisate, the politics, it's not my passion. And my sister is better at it than I am."

"It's pretty big of you to admit that."

"It's the truth. A strong woman doesn't detract from my masculinity. If that was the case, then I would not be here with you."

"You brought me here to meet your sister?"

"No. I brought you here to show you my secrets. You showed me your magic tricks, I'll show you mine."

He gave her a tug. She came easily, seeming content to let him take the lead while she followed at his side.

"You know all castles were built to defend and protect the people behind the walls."

Omar slipped an arm around her. A *whoop whoop* sound bounced off the walls. He knew the helicopter was parked above. It wouldn't leave until they were ready to depart. So, it could only be his heart pounding as it soared with Lark in his arms.

"See those stone circles, they are basically an obstacle course. They're meant to slow the invaders down, but the patient man will make his way through."

He linked their fingers together. His fingertips tingled. A shiver of pleasure rolled down his spine, like a cool breeze on a summer's night.

"Even the narrow stairwell was part of the defenses to avoid an attacker ..."

He pressed her against the wall. It was after hours, and most of the servants would be in their own quarters. The hall was empty, but the castle was not. Still, he no longer cared who saw them or what they might think. But he did not care for prying eyes.

"Inhabitants know the layout, which is the greatest advantage if an intruder breaches a wall."

Omar pressed her hand to the secret passage. The door opened. Now, he was the one with the trick up his sleeve.

"If all else fails, there's always a secret passageway."

A trap door opened, and he secreted her inside.

CHAPTER FOURTEEN

No one had ever made a candlelight dinner for her. Not only were they dining by flickering flame, but he'd found out her favorite foods and displayed them on what looked like a magic carpet, only it wasn't floating.

They sat on the ground on lush carpets. On serving dishes was beef bourguignon with a buttery wine sauce, the fluffiest potatoes Lark had ever sunk a fork into, and a leek vinaigrette that melted on her tongue. For dessert, she was treated to a slice of raspberry clafoutis. The traditional dish was always made with cherries, but her dad had always swapped out the pitted sweets for raspberries.

How had Omar known that? He'd probably grilled Spin. When Lark got back to Mondego

House, she'd have to squeeze the life out of her best friend in thanks. That is if she made it back to Mondego House tonight.

Omar kept his distance in the secluded room. Not that there was much space between them. It would take nothing for him to reach out and take her.

The flame in his gaze told Lark he wanted to. The curl of his lips told her he was hungry for the dish across the room from him more than he was for the one on his plate. But instead of taking a bite out of her, he toyed with his wine glass.

Lark reached out toward him. Omar's smile grew as her fingers got closer. A flame from the candlelight danced in the dark of his eyes. She spread her fingers and snatched that flame.

They weren't cast in darkness, not with the dozens of flickering lights illuminating the small space. Tendrils of smoke rose from the extinguished flame. The tendrils wrapped around Lark's wrist like a bracelet.

With her other hand, she picked up another candle. She brought that flame into the wisps of smoke from the candle she'd extinguished. Without ever touching the wick of the first candle, Lark brought the first flame back to life.

Omar reached out then. He took the second candle from her hand. He blew the light out and then pressed a kiss to each of her fingers. With each brush of his lips, Lark felt a light ignite inside of her.

"Aren't you going to ask me how I did that trick?" she said.

"No," he said around a mouthful of her index finger. "I'm under no illusions about you."

"No?"

"You're the real deal."

He came onto his knees. Leaning into her, he brushed a light kiss across her lips. It wasn't enough.

Lark leaned forward. But instead of his lips, she met with something only slightly sweeter. The clafoutis.

He grinned as he fed her a bit. Using his thumb, he wiped a spot of the treat from the corner of her mouth and licked his finger. Clearly, the man liked to play with his food.

"I still don't understand why there are so few female magicians in the world," said Omar.

"The only place you won't find a line at a magician show is the ladies room," said Lark. "We're an oddity."

"I find you fascinating."

He could've leaned over and taken her lips again.

She would've given them. Instead, Omar savored his wine, not taking his eyes off her mouth, making her feel thirsty, hungry, wanton.

She'd been seduced but not out of her clothes. Omar had methodically and meticulously unlocked every one of her defenses as though she were a castle, and he'd taken apart all of her booby-traps.

"There's a stigma against women practicing magic," said Lark. "Trials, stakes, fires. Throughout history, if a woman possesses special powers, she was likely persecuted. Even midwives, healers, fortunetellers."

"Can you tell the future?"

"Yours? Sure." She leaned in closer. "The future is that you're going to fall for me."

Omar shook his head. "That's the present."

Lark felt something shift in her chest. Her thoughts scattered. The raspberries he'd just fed her were like a triple shot of espresso waking all her senses. Every nerve ending stirred as though from a deep slumber.

She felt herself drifting to him. The pull irresistible. She was completely under his spell. She was also certain she was about to be seduced out of her clothes now.

"Are we keeping women now?"

Instead of tasting the sweet wine on Omar's lips, Lark felt the bitter taste from the sigh that escaped his mouth. They both turned to find they were no longer alone in their secret hideaway.

The woman standing in the doorway could've passed for a model. But not one of the carbon copies that walked New York catwalks. No, this woman would've graced the international stages with her dark hair, golden brown features, and intelligent gaze. Lark knew she should be intimidated by this beauty. But the resemblance was too stark for jealousy to creep in.

"You're supposed to be in the capital, Alana," said Omar.

"I was. But only for the day. Yesterday."

"Yesterday?" Omar sat up. He angled his forearm to see his watch in the candlelight.

The two of them had talked all night and into the next day. And yet, Lark felt not an ounce of tiredness.

"You haven't brought a girl home in a long time," said Alana.

Lark felt pleased with that.

"And you are both still fully clothed," Alana continued. "I'm intrigued."

Lark stuck out her hand. "I'm Lark."

Alana ignored her hand and grinned a very familiar grin. "I know you are."

Alana slid a sly glance to her brother. Omar made a face that only a brother could give a sister when he wanted her to keep her mouth shut.

"Good to meet you." Alana took Lark's hand then. "I can't wait to see your show."

"I have an early morning meeting," Omar said, breaking the two apart and ushering Lark out of the room. "I can just make it if we leave now."

The copter ride was just as dazzling during the day as it had been at night. But the blades of the metal bird couldn't lift Lark any higher than the last kiss Omar gave her before he stepped out of the town car.

As he walked into the building, Lark saw his assistant come up the street. Marlena carried a tray of coffee cups in her hand. Her gaze went between her boss' back as he went into the building, and Lark as she rested her elbows on the open car door window.

"Good morning, Marlena," Lark said. There was no sense in hiding from his assistant. Besides, the two of them would likely be seeing a lot of each other under the circumstances. Lark might as well make a friend of the woman.

Marlena curled her lip and tilted up her nose. "It's nearly noon."

So, they wouldn't be besties. Okay. Lark knew it was best to nip this attitude in the bud so they could at least have a good working relationship.

"Marlena, is there something you want to say to me?"

"It's not worth it. I have far too much work to do than to give you a woman's liberation lesson."

The personal assistant didn't give the former magician's assistant a chance to make her case, which was that Lark didn't get her deal by laying on her back. She'd worked for her shot. She just so happened to trip up and fall for her boss.

But it was too late. Marlena had already turned on her sensible shoes and was headed into the building on a high horse.

CHAPTER FIFTEEN

As a member of the wedding party, Omar was on duty for hours before he had time to play. Hours had passed, and yet, here he was, still on duty, trying to wrangle the groomzilla better known to his unwitting subjects as the King of Córdoba.

"The knot of this tie is crooked."

"No, it's straight," said Omar. "Daniel already measured it with a ruler."

"Well, it's gone crooked since then." Leo undid the knot for the twentieth time and began meticulously retying it.

His groomsmen left him to it. Better he stayed occupied with the tie than take another peek out into the cathedral. Already, he'd complained that the lighting was too dim in the ancient building which was mainly lit by sunlight filtering through the stained glass windows.

Oh, and those windows? Leo felt the colors they'd been stained with hundreds of years ago were far too spring-like for his fall wedding. His Majesty gave a blank stare when he was told there was nothing to be done about it. That's when Omar had pointed out the crookedness of his tie.

"Is this a spot on my vest?" Leo asked, pinching the fabric of his jacket where a nonexistent spot lay.

But Omar was no longer paying attention to his monster of a best friend. His gaze had turned to the hall filling with people. One person in particular.

Lark was a vision in lilac. The light fabric hung from her shoulders like petals, softly blowing in the breeze. Her skirts pooled around her shapely stem-like legs, swaying with each of her steps. That confirmed it. The woman truly was a magical fairy.

He was walking toward her before his brain gave his feet command. But he didn't get far. A strong hand held him in place.

"Aren't you two keeping a low profile?" Daniel gripped his shoulder while also peeking his head out to get a look at Lark.

Omar was surprised the earl knew anything

happening in society. Daniel didn't pay attention to much outside of books. His green eyes gave Lark a once over. There was no male appreciation there. She was a real live girl with curves and not on a page written in san serif letters.

"I thought you gave up on performers," Daniel continued.

Omar looked back at the one performer who made his heart dance. "She's different."

"She looks like the rest of them."

"She's exquisite, and Lark has actual talent."

"So did Summer. And she still used you."

True, Summer had had talent. But she didn't use it much. She preferred to get by on the backs of others, which was why her ascent into the stars had stalled.

"Lark is different," Omar proclaimed proudly.

"You said that already."

"Well, she is. She's a hard worker. She's honest and strong-willed, and entirely capable. She doesn't need me to succeed. She's capable of doing it all on her own."

"That is different," said Daniel. "Yet, she's still snogging the boss."

Omar was done with the conversation. Daniel knew nothing of real relationships. His only experience was in fictional worlds of a time gone by.

Omar turned his attention back to the woman who had captivated him. It took him a moment to find her again. People were still filling into the cathedral, taking a moment to mingle and network before the show began.

The royal wedding was the place to be and be seen. The nobility took the opportunity to make inroads with other families, to shun old enemies, and to reinforce ancient bonds. But the high class weren't the only invitees.

The nouveau riche and new upper class were also in the mix. Captains of digital industry mixed amongst the blue bloods. Wet nosed politicians sniffed around for opportunity.

Finally, Omar spotted Lark again. She was smiling brightly. Her head was bent down to the Duchess of Mondego. The two women were grinning and giggling like school girls.

Many people came up to the two women. Noble class, nouveau riche, and commoner alike. Nian de Bernadino had always been a gracious, though quiet, noblewoman. These days, with her husband no longer looming over her, she had taken a new lease on life. She shook hands and spoke up to everyone who greeted her.

Lark stood at her side like a watchful guard post. The fact that Lark was protective and not opportunistic made Omar want her even more. He ached to take another step, all of the steps, that would lead him to her. But he held his place and did his duty.

Before he turned back to the groom who was now fussing with his cufflinks, Omar felt a chilled gust come through the hall. Looking over, he saw a ghost of the past. Summer swept into the hall on the arm of the man she'd left Omar for; Roberto Rancik.

Omar stood frozen as the two made their way over to the Duchess and Lark. When Rancik slithered up to Omar's new star, the marquis made to step forward. But once again, he was held back by Daniel.

"Let's not cause a scene," Daniel said. "If she is who you say she is, then there is nothing to worry about."

Omar grit his teeth as he watched the shady producer bow to the Duchess. Then he turned his greedy gaze to Lark. Nian's lips moved. Her huge smile had gone dim. She waved her hand between Rancik and Lark, making introductions.

Lark's once polite and indulgent smile stiffened after Nian's lips stopped moving. Perhaps she recognized Rancik's name. Lark's gaze slid to Summer and then back to Rancik, and her smile slipped all together.

Rancik was either ignorant or undaunted. He reached for Lark's hand, which she lifted slowly, reluctantly. As Rancik bent over her knuckles, Lark's lips curled in distaste.

Omar's heart soared. He turned to Daniel with a smirk of triumph. Daniel's head tilted slightly, giving only a hint of mollification.

This was a victory for Omar. He wanted to pump his fists into the air. He wanted to run up to Lark and lift her into his arms. She saw into Rancik. She recognized the snake he was. But Rancik wasn't done.

As the producer pulled away from Lark, Omar saw a flash of white between his hands. The object was the size of a business card. Rancik stuck out his elbow for Summer. Summer sneered over her shoulder at Lark who smiled serenely.

Once the producer and his fading star had gone, Lark waited for the Duchess to take her seat in the pews. With a flutter of her hands, Lark let the business card slip through her fingers and fall to the floor. Then for good measure, she toed the offensive scrap of trash away.

Omar felt like her toe had kick started his heart. The act of her toeing away Rancik's business card made him feel as though he'd fallen to the floor. He had fallen. He'd fallen hard for Lark Voorheen.

CHAPTER SIXTEEN

*O*mar didn't take his eyes off her the entire ceremony. Lark felt pinned in place by the best man's gaze. When the king said his vows, Lark felt certain she heard the words and Omar's voice. When Omar handed the king the sparkling ring, Lark had a vision of the marquis handing a ring to her.

She'd dreamed of getting married as a little girl. But the thought, the fantasy, hadn't crossed her mind in years. Definitely not since she'd stepped into the glittery shadows behind magicians.

For years, she'd been dancing in the dark where no one could see her talent. Omar al Shariff had given her a spotlight. He didn't ask for any of the shine to spill on to him. He was happy to stand in the background and watch her sparkle.

That's why when he came to her at the reception and swept her into his arms, she was so dazzled.

"Hey," he said.

"Hey," she parroted.

"I've made a decision."

"You have?"

"Hmm," he nodded. "I can't do this."

He spun her in his arms. Away from the warmth of his body, Lark felt desolate and cold. He held her only by her fingertips, and she resisted the urge to claw her way back to him. She hadn't needed to. Just as quickly as he spun her away, she was back inside his embrace.

"I can't hide us anymore," he said, gazing down at her with a bright light of care in his dark eyes. "We're coming out of the closet. Or from the back of the stage. Whatever. I don't care."

His large hands slid down to the small of her back. He pressed her to him in a possessive hold for all to see.

"All I know," Omar continued, "is that I have been in the same room with you for an hour, and I haven't kissed you. It was the hardest performance of my life. There won't be a repeat show."

"What are you saying?" She knew what he was saying, but she wanted it spelled out, spoken out loud.

"I'm saying that I'm going to kiss you senseless in front of the entire noble class of Córdoba, its citizens, and the press."

"Oh." Well, that made it crystal clear.

Omar's gaze locked on her lips, but he didn't press forward. Even though he'd made the decision, he was still waiting for her permission. God, this man.

"There is one thing," said Lark. "The Duchess."

"I'm dumping you, my dear," said the Duchess Mondego from behind her. Nian swayed in her son's arms.

"Don't break her heart," said Zhi. "She knows how to make a man disappear."

Lark giggled at the mother and son duo. When she turned back to Omar, she was met first by his lower lip and then his upper lip. Time stopped, and the music went mute all around her as Omar claimed her mouth in the midst of the dancing crowd.

It was the flashes of light that finally brought Lark back to her senses. From around the room, cameras caught their embrace. Omar held her tight but didn't hold back as they danced. Lark forgot to care what people might think of her. Marlena's glare and terse words were way off in the distance as Omar spun her round and round the dance floor.

He held her tight, letting her know that he had her back. That mattered more than others who were prepared to stomp all over it. Anytime Omar spun her away, he left his hand suspended in the air with the knowledge she'd come back to him. And she did with each change of beat, with each new song. Until he had to return to his duty and give the best man's speech.

"I was chosen to give this speech because I'm the brother Leo never had," said Omar from his place on the raised platform.

The crowd chuckled, all eyes turning to Prince Alex, who simply rolled his eyes and waved his hand magnanimously for Omar to continue.

"Truly, we are a lucky nation to have such a duty-bound king. Leo put his heart aside for years to take care of us. But the first time I saw him and Esme together, I knew we were in trouble."

Again, a light chuckle breezed through the crowd as their gazes turned to their new queen. Esme hadn't stopped beaming since Leo had lifted the veil from her face. The two were truly in love.

"The saying goes that a great flame follows a little spark. Well, I saw a spark in my friend's eyes that day. By the next day, we all saw the flames."

Nods of assent went through the crowd of family, friends, and well-wishers. Omar turned to the queen and addressed her directly.

"Esme, you radiate warmth. You made us all believe in love. This union will burn bright for our country. To Leo and Esme." Omar raised his glass. "May you find joy in each other, and may your flame burn bright for a lifetime of warmth and happiness."

After the crowd toasted and sipped their wine, Lark ducked into the ladies' room. She was not alone, of course. Spin and Jan accompanied her.

"Omar's speech was amazing," said Jan. "I've never seen him so romantic."

"I bet that has something to do with a certain magician," said Spin.

"I sense wedding bells in both your futures." Jan winked at Lark. The soon to be princess's own diamond ring sparkled back from the vanity mirror.

But in the mirror, both Spin and Lark's smiles dimmed. Taking in the sight of the two deer in headlights, the pie maker laughed.

"This will be a good show," said Jan. "Watching the two of you duck and dodge two men who are dead set on keeping you and settling down with you."

"Who said I was going to dodge?" said Spin as she reapplied gloss to her lips.

Only Lark was left unsmiling as she looked at the reflection of her commitment-phobic friend.

"Has he –?" asked Lark.

"No." Spin shook her head. "But he has been acting especially weird lately. I'm sure it's coming soon. And Jan's right, you'll probably be next."

"Omar and I just started dating. We haven't even ..." She wasn't about to confirm or deny out loud that they'd slept together. They'd only been on two dates. Three if you count their time on the dance floor. "Well, we haven't done much of anything."

"Neither had Alex and I," said Jan. "It's something about this place, American girls."

"I'm only half American," said Lark.

"That's all it takes," said Jan. "I give you until the end of the week," Jan said to Spin. "I would've given you a couple of months," Jan said to Lark. "But after that speech and your moves on the dance floor, honey, your days are numbered."

It should've freaked Lark out. The fact that it hadn't was what actually made her sweat.

"I'll be out in a sec," said Lark. "I just need to fix my face."

The two women linked arms and left her to her own reflection. Lark stared at herself in the mirror for a long moment. All the while, her heart thumped erratically. Was that pounding for Omar? Did she want it to be?

One of the stall doors opened. Lark hadn't realized anyone else had been present during their girl chat. Not that the bathroom was their private space. Lark really needed to fix her face when she saw who the eavesdropper was.

"You're a fool if you think he'll marry you," said Summer. Her eyes blazed with fury and a wash of jealousy, outlined in a smoky eye of envy.

"It's none of your business," said Lark.

"You're just business to him. Get that in your head, and you'll get ahead."

Lark wanted to rail against the woman. She wanted to tell her that Omar was more than his profession. He was a good man, a loyal man who joyed in other's success. He was a man not intimidated by a strong woman.

But something made Lark pause. She looked at Omar's former protégé and lover. All performers had a fire behind their eyes, a desire to run for their dream. The spark was gone from Summer's gaze.

"If you sign with Rancik, he can take you further than Omar can."

"Like he did you?"

Summer looked away, her eyes dulling even more. When she looked back, her gaze was full of flint. The kind of lead used in a pencil which looked tough, but easily scratched away when it was put under pressure.

"I've moved beyond performing now," said Summer. "Now, I'm scouting talent."

"Instead of showcasing your own."

Now, Lark understood why there was no more spark. Summer hadn't ever had any talent of her own. She wouldn't have gotten anywhere had it not been for Omar. She wasn't going anywhere else without using someone else's talent. That was all Lark needed to know.

"Omar is my partner," said Lark. "I'm not looking to go anywhere without him."

"Then, you'll fail."

"I doubt it. We make a strong team. And if we did fail, I know he'd catch me."

Lark didn't care to hear more. She didn't care

what this woman thought. She didn't care what anyone thought. She knew who she was and what she wanted. And she was going back out in the crowd of onlookers to get him.

The word gentlemen's club had a different connotation in this day than in the Victorian age. Now, those words evoked an establishment tucked away in a less than savory part of a city, filled with sketchy men, cloaked in shadows and raining down single currency bills on the gyrating and sparsely clad women on display.

The Garrison club was not such an establishment.

The centuries-old club had passed down the air of exclusivity. Unless you bled blue, you wouldn't get past the threshold. Prejudice still shaded the fixtures as no women were allowed inside the hall ... for now. But the sketchy and shady bunch somehow made it past the velvet ropes.

"Have you been here all night?" Lord Panek pulled at the tie that had been tight around his neck. He tossed the strip of fabric along with his coat onto the floor, certain one of the staff would come and pick it up.

"Can't go home," said Lord Romero. "The wife is angry."

Lord Romero sat in a plush robe and slippers. His thinning hair was wet. He clutched a thick cigar between his index and middle finger.

"Go to your mistress then," offered Panek as he slumped down next to the other man.

"Can't." Romero shook his head. Puffing on the cigar, he blew out tiny smoke circles. "She's angry I went and saw my wife."

The Garrison offered lodgings for members who paid extra on their membership. Many men did. The club was better than a full-service hotel in that it offered all the amenities for a long stay, the additional exclusivity, and the utmost discretion for the noblemen who played in these halls. Although free earbuds would be a nice addition to the excellent service. Or separate rooms for the lower dregs of the upper-class society.

Omar turned his body away from the other two men. There were less than ten members in the gathering room that morning. Omar didn't frequent the club as much as he had done in his youth. He'd long since grown weary of the company kept there. The only reason he'd stopped in that morning was to pass time before he could see Lark. That, and to catch up with Daniel who preferred the old world tradition of the gentleman's club.

Being on the outskirts of town, the club was closer to Mondego House where Omar was due in a few hours. He hadn't wanted to arrive early and look too eager, although that is exactly what he was. He was eager to see her, to hold her, to kiss her, to simply be with her.

"I should've been like the marquise here," Romero was saying. "I should've stayed a bachelor and vowed never to marry."

Omar lifted his head from the morning paper. "I made no such vow."

"No?" Romero turned to him, uncrossing his legs.

Omar cursed under his breath and looked away before he got too much of a show with the loose robe.

"Maybe you didn't say it out loud," Panek chimed in. "But it's clear by the lifestyle you chose for yourself."

Omar opened his mouth to argue. Then he closed his lips. Had he chosen a bachelor lifestyle? No. Not consciously anyway.

He had nothing against marriage. If it were to the right woman. He just hadn't met her in all his years. For years, his life had been inundated with performers, actresses, and women who were models and not their real selves.

None of them had been brimming with talent that made him see stars. None of them had brought something to the table to share with his good store and not simply take. None of them had invaded his every waking thought.

Until now.

Omar was not surprised when Lark's face appeared in his mind. He was nowhere near ready to ask the woman to marry him. But the thought of his future featured her prominently.

He harbored a clear vision of Lark standing by his side. Lark standing in front of him in the spotlight. Lark standing behind him during a storm they would weather together.

"Yes," Lord Romero picked up the thread. "We should've taken pointers from him. We should have made it clear that marriage was off the table and then sleep with whomever we chose."

Omar was well aware that was his reputation. With every new starlet he found, with every new talent he scouted, the press looked to make a connection with him and whatever pair of legs he presented to the world. It was not the truth. But men like Romero and Panek wouldn't hear or wouldn't care about the truth.

"What we should have done is open a business that has a lot of women in it, along with a plush couch in our offices, if you know what I mean." Panek waggled his eyebrows, making his meaning grossly clear.

"That was quite brilliant of you, Navarre," said Romero, twirling the stub of the cigar between his fingers. "Maybe it's not too late. I've got the money to start a modeling agency."

"Especially with that new bit of talent you brought on," said Panek. "The brunette from the wedding. Did you see the legs on that one?"

"Didn't make it that far south," said Romero. "Those breasts were –"

The man flew across the room. His legs went over his head. His robe fell from his torso giving everyone an unwanted eyeful.

"Keep her name out of your mouth," Omar said as he stood over the man. His fists opened and clenched, aching for the idiot to say something more so that he could take another shot.

"What's your problem?" Romero pulled his robe over his family jewels. "She's just another piece of -"

Omar's fists flew toward the man's foul mouth. Unfortunately, there wasn't a connection. Something held him back.

He knew it couldn't be Panek. The man was a toothpick and a coward. He was also nowhere to be found. It was Daniel holding Omar back. The large pacifist with a penchant for swordplay was the only man in the room who could.

"Let's take a walk," said Daniel. "It smells in here."

It took the Earl a solid minute to get Omar to turn around and walk out of the room. Omar stuttered down the steps, his feet listening to his fists that wanted another shot. But Daniel blocked his way. Once in the cool air, Omar took his first deep breath.

"What was that about?" said Daniel.

"You heard what they said about Lark."

Daniel shrugged. "It isn't the first, or the last time someone will disparage the current woman you're with."

"She's not current," Omar shouted.

"So, you've already thrown her over then."

Omar frowned at his friend and his use of out of date slang. "No, I haven't broken up with her. I don't want to throw her anywhere. I want to keep her."

"Oh?" Daniel's brows lifted high. "That's different."

"I told you, she's different."

"It's a classic case of Jane Eyre."

Omar rolled his eyes and pinched the bridge of his nose. He was not in the mood for one of Daniel's book reports.

"The hired help who wins the heart of the boss. But they can't marry on account of his insane first wife, so he makes Jane a deal that they can live together in secret."

Omar groaned. These talks with Daniel had been great back in university when he hadn't wanted to read the books. Daniel would offer just enough detail so that Omar could write his papers and get decent grades.

"Oh," said Daniel. "I'm sorry? Did you not read that one? Did I spoil it for you?"

"I'm not married to a crazy woman." Though he did have a crazy, interfering ex. But Summer wasn't stopping him from being with Lark. "I don't want to hide what I feel for Lark. I want a future with her."

He took off toward his car. Once inside, he stomped on the gas. He no longer cared what anyone thought. He no longer wanted to wait. He was eager to see the woman who had captured his heart.

CHAPTER EIGHTEEN

"Girls can't do magic."

Lark inhaled, doing her best to hold her smile. But if the little man looked closely, he'd see it in her eyes. He'd see that he was this close to her stuffing his ninety-pound little body into a hat.

But she couldn't do that. She wouldn't. He was a child. Best way to handle children was to teach them a lesson.

Lark turned from the prejudiced little nit to the ire of his attention. The young girl had her head cast down, her gaze averted. The wand in her hand trembled as though any magic gathered there was fizzling out. Her lower lips twisted as though she could no longer give voice to the silly, complicated words used to evoke magic.

The Duchess had invited Lark to teach the school kids a couple of magic tricks as a treat. There were mostly boys in the room. After that remark, the other two girls quietly slipped out the door, leaving the one holding the trembling wand. The girl lifted her gaze then, eyed the door as though she wanted to disappear out of it.

Lark put herself between the door and the would-be magician. The only thing that would be vanishing today would be her lack of self-confidence.

"All right, everyone," Lark said to the crowded room of kids. "Who's ready to make a coin disappear?"

There were a number of excited MEs. But also a few groans.

"A coin?" grumbled the little chauvinist in training. "My grandpa can do that. I told you she wasn't a real magician. She's a girl."

"Actually, little man, I'm a grown woman. I'm also the most clever person in the room."

He quirked a doubtful eyebrow.

"Watch and learn."

Lark straightened to find a few more doubtful

brows lifted. Here she was again; a girl surrounded by males who thought they knew more than her. She'd had to fight so hard for every trick. She'd studied this craft from the history to the technical, to the science, to the showmanship. Meanwhile, all the gatekeepers had cared about was whether or not she could fit inside a trick box to be sawed in half. Or if her costume was snug enough to distract from their sleight of hand.

Well, no more.

Magic was where she'd found her confidence. More than anything, she wanted to teach that particular trick to the self-conscious little girl whose dreams were leaking out of the corner of her eyes.

"Everyone grab a coin," said Lark.

The boys all rushed to the table where an array of Córdovian coins lay. They jostled each other for the first pick, even though the coins were all the same. The girl waited on the sidelines for her turn.

Lark took the few steps over to her. She smiled down at the girl and offered her a coin from her pocket. This coin was different. It was special.

"Here," said Lark. "You can use mine."

The girl put her wand away. Then she reached out her hands for the coin. Lark placed the coin in the center of the girl's palm.

"What's your name?" asked Lark.

"Luisa, but everyone calls me Lulu."

"Lulu, is it? Did you know that's the name of a famous female magician?"

Lulu's eyes went wide. Her lip stopped trembling and formed an O of wonder.

"It's true. Laughing Lulu performed magic tricks where she'd lift more than one man up from the ground."

"Girls can't do that," Lulu whispered.

"Hmmm," was Lark's noncommittal response. "But magician's can."

Lark grinned at the girl, then gave her a wink. Lulu's smile grew wider, with a hint of more confidence.

"All right," Lark said, turning back to the boys. "You've got your coins?"

They all held up the coins.

Lark explained the steps to make the coin disappear. The trick was quite simple, but the young men asked copious amounts of questions. Many having nothing to do with the task in their hands.

"Can I make my brother disappear?"

"Can I make my math teacher disappear?"

"Can I make a dragon appear?"

"Is everybody ready?" Lark shouted over them,

cutting off the tirade of questions. "It's time to say the magic words."

"*Expelliarmus.*"

Abracadabra was so last generation.

Nearly all the coins clattered to the ground. Except one. Lulu held up empty hands. Her fingers were steady. Her eyes were bright with triumph.

"Whoa," came a chorus of appreciation from the boys.

"How'd you do that?" said the loudmouth who had been so certain a moment ago that magic was no place for girls. He stepped over his coin and came up to her.

"I just followed the instructions," said Lulu.

That was the trick about magic. It was all mostly a set of instructions to be followed. Follow the right sequence, and it worked like magic. That, and having the right sized coin.

Typically, girls' hands were smaller than most men's. Lulu would've never been able to perform the coin trick with one of the regular sized coins. The instructions had been the same, but Lark had given her an advantage because of her sex.

With a flick of her wrists, Lulu made the coin reappear. Lark hadn't taught that bit yet. But if a smart person simply reverse-engineered the trick, it was pretty much common sense.

The boys cheered. They shoved the naysayer out of the way to get to Lulu. Many asked for her help. At the end of class, Lulu came over to Lark to hand back the coin.

"Keep it."

Lulu's face lit up like the inside of a wand. "I love magic. But my mom wants me to be practical, to become something like a lawyer or doctor."

"The law and medicine are a kind of magic," said Lark. "Lawyers can free people from imprisoment, and doctors perform medical miracles every day. But real magic is better."

"I didn't know girls could be magicians. Just assistants that men put into a box and cut in half."

"It's all just an illusion. The assistant does all the work."

"Sounds about right," Lulu said, rolling her eyes at the young boys filing out of the room.

"Not all guys are bad," said Lark. "Most of them aren't, to be honest."

Lark had found herself one of the good ones in Omar. He hadn't once tried to stuff her in a box or cut her in half. He made her sparkle from the inside out. And he was all too happy to give her the entire spotlight.

Never had she been with a man who made her feel that way. She doubted there was anyone else like him out there. At least not a man who wasn't taken. The Nobles of Córdoba were a different breed.

Walking into the great room where she would be meeting Omar later that night, she saw two other nobles sitting next to the women who they'd given their hearts to.

"They are utter scum," growled Prince Alex.

The prince wore a scowl on his typically carefree face. Beside him sat Jan. Her jovial features were pulled with concern.

"Why can't they just leave well enough alone?" asked Zhi.

Lark was used to the duke's serious expressions. But there were angry lines at the corners of his mouth. Spin rested a hand on his arm as though she were pulling him back from a fight.

Lark looked in the direction of where all their gazes were trained. The sound of the television was loud now that the two men had quieted.

"The marquise has gone and done it again," said a familiar voice. Larked looked up to find the reporter-assistant from her showcase a few days ago. "He's found another mediocre talent with legs for days and bankrolled her. Lark Voorheen was suddenly catapulted from magician's assistant to a full-blown magician overnight after catching al Shariff's eye. Now, the citizens of Córdoba will have to suffer through another starlet whose only talent is on the casting couch."

"Don't listen," said Spin. Her hand was now on Lark's arm as though holding her back from a fight with the idiot box. "You know that's not the truth."

"She's right," said Jan, rising from her place beside Alex. "And when you get on that stage, the whole country will see the truth."

No, they wouldn't, Lark thought. That reporter had seen the truth with his own eyes. He'd experienced it, but he still preferred this storyline. Just as Marlena had seen Lark's hard work, but decided to believe Lark had gotten ahead on her back.

Lark should've known better. She should've done better. She knew that any hint of a relationship with her and her boss would be a disaster to her reputation, to her show, to her dream. But she'd thought she didn't need to follow the instructions.

The problem was she didn't want to give up

Omar. She also didn't want to give up her career. She was ready to slump down on the couch in defeat when an idea hit her. It was an idea she knew Omar wouldn't like. But she saw no other way up the ladder of success.

CHAPTER NINETEEN

The day had started out sunny, with a bright yellow sun shining down from a clear sky. However, by the time he'd pulled away from the club and onto the main road, the skies had tinted a foul shade of gray. The pit-pat of the rain only irritated him further as it slowed traffic on the way to his destination.

Omar knew he shouldn't let those two noble pieces of scum get to him. But they had struck a nerve. He knew how the industry worked. He knew how precious reputations were, especially when they were the reputations of women. Whatever people thought of his relationship with Lark, Omar knew he'd emerge unscathed.

Even if he was whispered about behind cupped

hands or across the television, he'd still come out on the other end with little injury to his character. There had been a little talk after his affair with Summer. He'd gone on to grow his business and attract more clientele. Whereas her star had faded.

Truth be told, that was largely due to the fact that she had very little real talent. Lark was an entirely different story. Not only did she have talent, but he didn't want her to fade from his life.

He wanted to keep her.

Forever.

The clouds parted as the realization hit him. This was no passing fancy for him. His feelings for this woman would not dull or diminish. This was love.

Rain still fell when he pulled up to Mondego House. But the clouds had parted, and the sun was shining. Omar stepped out of his car and felt the droplets fall on his face. The rainwater washed his foul mood away. The sunshine warmed his beating heart.

It didn't matter what anyone thought of his relationship with Lark. What was between them was there to stay. He needed to find her and declare it.

Walking into the great room where all of his friends were seated was like walking into a wake.

Alex, never at a loss for words or a good quip, chewed at his bottom lip. Zhi's perpetually smiling face was set in a grimacing line. Jan and Spin were crowded around Lark. Both of the women glanced at Omar, then quickly looked away.

Worst of all, Lark wouldn't look up at him. What had he done? Had Daniel called and told them about his little skirmish at the club?

It was the television screen that broke the silence. Omar recognized the reporter. There was a wicked gleam to the man's eye, as though he was having the time of his life while kicking a little puppy just off camera. The reporter's words didn't matter. The images flashing on the screen spoke volumes.

They were all of Omar. On his arm was a parade of slender beauties. Snapshot after snapshot showed him with models, actresses, socialites, and the like.

The majority of the outings had been innocent. Most had been photo opportunities. On the women's part, not his. But he'd played along.

The last snapshot was of him and Lark. The reporting was scandalous, filled with lies. Every word uttered by the loathsome reporter was designed to prick and sting. And it was all Omar's fault.

Omar had hurt Lark just by loving her. The press would make a field day of their relationship. Her reputation as a magician was on a very shaky line.

He walked over to the television and turned it off. When he turned back to face this bit of music, the room was emptying of his friends. He was left alone with Lark.

Lark's fae-like features were weary. Her slender shoulders slumped, as though in defeat. Her elegant fingers twisted at her middle.

Omar stepped forward and captured her hands in his. "Lark, I'm so sorry."

Lark nodded, still not looking at him. Panic began to creep up his spine. Was he about to lose her? Would she choose to disassociate from him to save her career?

He couldn't ask her to do otherwise. They had only just met, only just started. He couldn't ask her to give up everything she was for him.

Oh, but how he wanted to.

Omar wanted to tell her not to worry about working. He wanted to tell her that he would take care of her. Yes, for the rest of her life.

But what kind of life would that be for a woman with magic in her blood? Already, much of her sparkle had gone out of her eyes. This had to be like watching a loved one die.

Finally, she lifted her gaze. "You're not gonna like what I have to say."

"Lark, we can fight this." He was willing to drop to his knees and beg if he had to.

She came into his arms and rested her head against his chest. Omar's arms clamped around her, determined she would never escape him, never escape them.

"The harder we fight," she said into his chest, "the more they'll come at us."

Us? She'd said us. "You're not giving up on us?"

She lifted her head, a frown marring her perfect brow. "No, I'm not giving up on us."

Relief flooded him like a deluge of rain emptying from a storm cloud.

"But." The way she punctuated the word sounded like a strike of lightning. "I am leaving you."

Omar looked down at her. Her eyes were clear, focused, determined. His confusion cleared as realization dawned. "You mean your show. You're leaving me as your producer."

"Yes," she confirmed. "I want us to be together as a couple. But not in business."

It shouldn't have hurt. But it did. He got the girl, just not the magician.

"Everyone thinks we're using each other," Lark continued. "We know we're not, but it's going to impact both of our businesses. So, let's get out of business with each other."

It made sense. It was the logical thing to do. He should've thought of it.

"I'm going to sign with Rancik Entertainment."

CHAPTER TWENTY

Her name was in lights. Large circular bulbs, shining neon bright in the early morning light of a new Córdovian day.

The buzzing was not only from the electric lights. There was a buzz all around her as she climbed out of Omar's town car and headed into the Medieval Theater owned by Roberto Rancik.

Camera lights flashed all around them as Omar handed her out of the car. He kept her close, ignoring the flashes surrounding them and questions shouted at them. Lark didn't try to leave his embrace. In his arms was the only calm place in the storm around them.

It had been a whirlwind the last couple of days

of signing with Rancik and moving the production to his theater across town. But it was all working out.

The press was having a field day with the story of a female magician and her two producers. Some of the stories bordered on the salacious, printing stories of Lark dating both men. A few of them went the romantic route with Omar as the hero, giving up his love interest to protect his reputation. Only one paper posited that it was Lark who had done it all as a smart business decision.

Neither Lark nor Omar bothered to correct them. Rancik spent his time lauding that he had stolen Omar's talent from him. Lark and Omar didn't correct that either. They both knew the truth. There were bound to be compromises along the way. Besides, all the firestorm of reporting had led to sold out tickets for the next three weeks.

But the best part of the deal? There was no longer any hiding how she felt about Omar. She could hold his hand in public. She could go to dinner with him or a take in a show and not worry how it would impact her career. She had successfully separated the two, and now she had it all.

"Final rehearsal," Omar said, pulling her in close. "Good luck today."

He brought her in for a kiss. It was just a light brush of his lips against hers. He'd given her a hundred such kisses in the past week, but each time it made her heart skip a beat and flutter down back in place.

The cameras ate it up. Splashed across the papers and the entertainment news were dozens of snapshots of them kissing, gazing at each other. Whenever Lark looked at those pictures, she saw a woman in love. Whenever she was in Omar's arms, she felt like a woman who had fallen.

Omar loosened his hold on her. Lark fought the urge to pull him back to her. She wanted to stay inside his embrace.

She'd seen the clouds move over his features when they'd pulled up outside the theater. But he'd held his tongue. Omar brushed a kiss across her knuckles, making her fingers tingle. Then he let her go and climbed inside the car. And then, with a wink, he was gone.

He never came inside the theater. She'd never asked him to. She knew this was hard for him. But not as hard as it was for her.

Walking into the theater, she was confronted again with the very real understanding that she had made a mistake. An egregious mistake. A colossal mistake.

Lark sighed as she walked into her dressing room. She eyed her new costume with utter disdain. It was skintight, full of sequins and sparkles and strategic cutouts that left nothing to the imagination. It was one of the first changes Roberto Rancik had requested now that it was his show. There were bound to be compromises along the way.

Turning at the huff coming from her doorway, Lark saw that Blaze had fared no better.

"It's a speedo," said the fake magician.

It was indeed a speedo. But on the bright side, at least she wasn't the only one being objectified. But what could she do?

Switching producers at the last minute had been her idea. She had to see this, and all of Rancik's changes, through. She just had to believe that the substance of her show would win the crowd over.

"I was thinking we should cut out the lecture bit about the history of magic at the top of the show," said the producer in question.

He stood center stage as Lark and Blaze made their way out. Summer stood behind him. There was a scowl on her beautiful face. Lark couldn't understand why the woman frowned. Wasn't this what she'd wanted? To get Lark away from Omar?

"People aren't coming for a history lesson," Rancik was saying. "They're coming to be entertained."

"The history bit sets up a lot of the tricks in the second act," said Lark. "Losing it would cut the show down to forty-five minutes."

"Perfect timing," said Rancik. "We could double the number of daily shows and add a matinee."

Lark's throat closed up. A show full of skin and no magical lectures. What had she done? Unfortunately, by the time she found her voice, Rancik was on the phone and exiting stage left.

"I told you," said Summer. "I told you Omar would tire of you, and you'd have to come crawling here."

"I didn't come crawling here," said Lark. "Omar drove me over."

"He drove you?" asked Summer. Her pretty face was contorted in confusion, and then pity. "That's cruel."

"He's picking me up, too. We're still together. We decided to separate the business and the personal."

"There's no such thing," said Summer.

Lark was tired of this particular lecture. She

signaled Blaze so that they could run through the show. She had to figure out how to make it work with this newest batch of changes. She couldn't complain. This was what she'd asked for. There were bound to be some compromises.

Only, every time they ran through each trick, the show seemed to get worse and more clunky. By quitting time, Lark was ready to curl into a ball and give up. But she couldn't.

She stepped out of the barely-there cat suit. Washed the glitter off her face. And pulled on a smile.

Omar was waiting for her when she walked out of the theater. Her heart skipped a beat when she saw him. He got off the phone when he saw her and opened his arms.

Lark tried not to cling and failed. Her fingers dug into his back. Her face burrowed into his chest.

"How did it go?" he asked.

"Fine," she lied. "Everything is great."

"Is that glitter on your hands?"

Lark brushed her hand on her jacket, but the sparkles didn't fade. Omar let it drop. As always, he didn't interfere with the show. He only sought ways to help her realize her dreams. Somehow, he knew that what she needed right now was to be inside his embrace.

He kissed her soundly. It was the fuel she needed. The reminder as to why she was doing this. She was going to have it all; the career and the man.

There would be some compromises along the way.

CHAPTER TWENTY-ONE

*P*ressing his lips to hers was the only magic show Omar cared about. He felt sawed in half, put back together, and levitated all at the same time when he was with Lark.

It had nearly torn him apart when she'd left him for Rancik. But she was right. Omar couldn't produce her and love her at the same time, not with the public hounding their every move and decision.

All attention should be focused on her talent. Once the press and the people saw what she could do in a performance, they'd relent and lose interest in her personal life. Or at least he hoped that's what would happen.

He could see the weariness setting into her pale eyes as she rested her head in the cradle of his shoulder. Yesterday, the wary look had only been at the corners of her eyes. Slowly, it was creeping in.

He wanted to peel back the layers, get her to tell him what troubled her. But he feared he knew what the answer would be; Rancik.

Omar's instincts screamed to protect her. To shove Rancik away from her spotlight so the man wouldn't dull her shine. But he couldn't do that. He knew Lark was capable. He needed her to know he believed she could handle herself.

Sometimes it stunk being an evolved man.

So, instead of coming to a rescue she likely didn't need and certainly didn't want, he wined her, dined her, and then twirled her around the dance floor of his club until her eyes were shining bright. By the time he dropped her at Mondego House early into the next morning, the weariness was gone from her shoulders. He kissed her soundly, then went home to catch a few hours of sleep before his day was set to begin.

"What should I do with the rest of Ms. Voorheen's things that were left in her dressing room?" said Marlena from behind her clipboard. "Donations?"

"No," Omar frowned. "Give them to me."

"If you're going to use them for your next little

affair, you should know women don't like re-gifts that belonged to the previous lover." She checked off a box on her list.

"What new affair?" he said. "I'll give them to Lark myself tonight after her show."

"You're still seeing her?"

"Of course. She's my girlfriend."

The clipboard clattered to the floor. "She's with Rancik, your rival."

"It was the best thing for our relationship."

"Relationship?"

"Lark is in my life. She will be around for a very long time. Forever, if I'm lucky."

That little confession felt good. He wanted to repeat it to everyone he met on the street. He figured he'd get a head start at opening night for her show.

Surprisingly, Omar wasn't the first of his friends to show up for the show. Alex and Jan sat with Princess Penelope between them in the royal box. Zhi's box was empty. Omar could see the Duke, Duchess, and Spin seating a group of kids from their school down in the first few rows.

There was magic in the air. A spark of energy traveled through the crowd as people couldn't keep still in their seats. Finally, the house lights dimmed. But the theater wasn't cast in darkness.

There were glitter and sparkles everywhere. The faux magician, Blaze Mercury, came out ... in a speedo.

Omar's stomach dropped. His gut high kicked bile into his chest, giving his heart acid burn. To say he got a bad feeling was an understatement.

Where was Lark? It was her banter on magic history and women in magic that was meant to open the show. Several tricks wouldn't work without that setup.

And then she appeared. Omar's knuckles turned white as he held himself in his seat. She was barely dressed.

Her gaze found him in the crowd. The sparkle there was fake. The smile was forced. She swallowed and turned from him to begin.

He'd seen enough. She'd given up her dream to be with him, and it had turned into a nightmare. Omar left his seat and stormed down the steps in a rage.

CHAPTER TWENTY-TWO

The show had no intermission. It was no longer long enough to warrant one. But still, he left. The one person in the audience Lark wanted to impress.

Omar had risen from his box seat and left before she'd even performed her first trick. Maybe it was the reimagined set Rancik had constructed? Or perhaps Blaze's speedo? Or the strategically placed sequins on her barely-there costume?

He could take his pick because Omar knew this wasn't her. Not who she was. Not who she wanted to be. Not what she wanted to do.

Lark ignored her cue from Blaze to begin the first trick. Her gaze fell on the front row of the audience. In the second row, she saw the little girl who wanted to be a magician herself. There was confusion on Lulu's brow as she watched Lark move center stage. The young girl held her wand in one hand and passed the coin Lark had given her between the fingers of her other hand. The hand that held the wand trembled.

Lark knew why. Men were still pulling the strings of her act. When Omar had taken up her show, he had never done that. He had handed over the reins happily. He'd believed in her vision. He'd supported her every step. And now look where she stood.

She was the one who had pulled the ride to a halt. All because it mattered to her how people thought she'd come on board the ride in the first place. Well, now she was here, standing center stage of her dreams.

She'd done it. But it meant nothing without the man she loved and his support. So it was time to go.

"For my final trick—"

"Don't you mean your first trick, assistant?" came Blaze's voice.

"I'm no one's assistant. I'm a magician. And I'll be performing a disappearing act."

"That's no longer part of the show," said Blaze.

The audience laughed, clearly thinking it was indeed part of the show.

And just like that, she had her audience back. Her entrance had been lackluster. But her exit would be memorable.

"There is no real magic in a disappearing act," she said. "The key, as with any illusion, is making the audience believe. Because you see, magic starts in the heart. Love is an unseen and elusive power. If you believe in love, then you know how to work magic."

She had no cape to hide behind. There was no furniture to slip around. There was just Lark, a woman in love and ready to show the world.

"I'm in love with Omar al Shariff, the Marquis of Navarre. He has been the solid footing beneath my wings that has allowed me to fly. Together we are going to soar."

She turned to the curtains off stage where Rancik stood.

"If you didn't catch that, Mr. Rancik, that was my notice."

Lark turned back to the crowd.

"Now, all I need is for you to say the magic word. Can you guess what that is?"

"Love," shouted a familiar voice.

Lark nodded at her best friend. Spin gave her two thumbs up. The crowd began to chant the word.

Lark pressed her hand to her heart. Flinging her hands in the air, she tossed up a spray of glitter and was gone.

Down she went into a tunnel of darkness. From above, she could hear the audience applauding. She also heard Blaze questioning where she went.

It wasn't a trick she'd taught him. It wasn't a trick she'd ever planned to use. But love had caught up to her with its own sleight of hand, and now Lark was under a spell she had no intention of unraveling.

She'd fallen. Hard. Not on her rear. She'd fallen standing up, eyes wide open, heart at the ready for Omar. She just had to go and find him.

Lark took a step back and bumped into an immovable wall. It beat in a fast-paced rhythm. The pattern of the heart beats matched her own.

She turned around beneath the trap door and there he was.

Omar waited with this arms opened wide. His brow had been pulled in displeasure, but that line was quickly easing away. Relief flushed his cheeks. Tenderness brightened his gaze.

"I'm so sorry," they both said at the same time.

Omar wrapped his arms around her, holding her

tight. If she planned to disappear again, she'd have to take him with her. Lark made no move to go. She wrapped her arms around him and clasped her hands at his neck.

"You first," he said. "Why are you sorry?"

"The show was a disaster."

He neither agreed or disagreed.

"My vision got lost, not because of Rancik; it was because of me. Because I was so concerned about what other people would think. I didn't want my personal life to interfere with my professional life. But when I'm with you, you make me shine."

"Easiest job I ever had," he said.

"Will you take me back?"

"I never let you go."

"I meant my show. Will you take me back as a business partner?"

"I never took your name down from the marquee," he said. "Your name is in lights on my theater, just as it's blazed across my heart."

"I told you your future," she said. "I forgot to mention that it was mine too. I've fallen hard for you."

"Don't worry. I'll always make sure there's a cushion where you land."

Lark looked over to the side where the mattress

beneath the trap door had been perfectly lined up. Then she turned back to the man who made her heart turn tricks.

Omar brought his lips to hers in a firework of a kiss that made her see stars. What was between them was no illusion. It was pure. It was magic.

Shanae Johnson was raised by Saturday Morning cartoons and After School Specials. She still doesn't understand why there isn't a life lesson that ties the issues of the day together just before bedtime. While she's still waiting for the meaning of it all, she writes stories to try and figure it all out. Her books are wholesome and sweet, but her heroes are hot and heroines are full of sass!

And by the way, the E elongates the A. So it's pronounced Shan-aaaaaaaa. Perfect for a hero to call out across the moors, or up to a balcony, or to blare outside her window on a boombox. If you hear him calling her name, please send him her way!

You can sign up for Shanae's Reader Group at http://bit.ly/ShanaeJohnsonReaders

The Rebel Royals series

The King and the Kindergarten Teacher

The Prince and the Pie Maker

The Duke and the DJ

The Marquis and the Magician's Assistant

The Princess and the Principal